# WUSHU MOON MAGIC

J. HAND

## SHIRES PRESS

4869 Main Street
P.O. Box 2200
Manchester Center, VT 05255
www.northshire.com/printondemand.php

Wushu Moon Magic
http://www.wushumoonmagic.com
©2009 Julie Hand
All rights reserved

ISBN Number: 978-1-60571-0421-6
Library of Congress Number: 2009909681

### NORTHSHIRE BOOKSTORE

***Building Community, One Book at a Time***

*This book was printed at the Northshire Bookstore, a family-owned, independent bookstore in Manchester Ctr., Vermont, since 1976. We are committed to excellence in bookselling. The Northshire Bookstore's mission is to serve as a resource for information, ideas, and entertainment while honoring the needs of customers, staff, and community.*

*Printed in the United States of America
using an Espresso Book Machine from On Demand Books*

a note about writing wushu moon magic:

when i returned to my roots in vermont just over one year ago, my intention was to write a nonfiction book about a long walk. as you'll see, this is definitively not that book. yet as i was reminded today—September 13, 2009— nothing is a coincidence in life, and my first 48 hours at home last year were indicative of the fact that fiction would be my fodder.

so a little about writing wushu...before dinner the second eve at my mom's house last summer i stumbled upon a book she kept from her high school days about writing fiction. i browsed a few pages but the brown book was musty and made me sneeze, so i set it down.

over the course of the past year, i wove words in and out of journals, letters, and emails. but it wasn't until march 9th this past spring that i truly got cranking again. surprisingly i moved through a first draft relatively easily and by april 30th, i had 300 pages. however when i reread what i had written, i realized it wasn't the story my heart longed to tell. though i wasn't sure what was...

fortunately i found ten pages buried deep in those 300 that held the faint embers of what i was after, so i extracted them and started anew. i finished a second draft—those ten pages plus 200 more—by the end of may. finally by june 15th, i had completed a third draft and thought—yes, at least i can "work" with this.

then a funny thing happened as i squared up to the table to dig into the text for a final round. my own ghosts of a very real kind came whizzing back at breakneck speed. presumably, confronting my own little demons and writing about byrd's simultaneously was a strange twist of fate. yet i believe there's more to it than that.

the ironic scenario brought me face to face with the truth about writing fiction. while nearly anything flies in a 'made-up' tale, the words must hang together in some coherent fashion to 'ring true' [mom's book told me that last summer].

so facing my own ghosts in the real world as i faced byrd's on the page, i was forced to ask myself a serious question. were the words of this book ones I believed in? did they ring true to me? if i were byrd, could i stand by them? again, digging deep [thanks ghosts], the answer is yes.

here is one more reason why—this book is about a photographer who goes on an assignment in search of the magic of the moon. sitting at the dorset quarry today, penning my final thoughts, a couple from canada approached me. they had a camera and a dog in tote. "would you be so kind as to take our picture?" they asked. not a problem. i stood up and asked if they'd like their dog in the frame as well. "no, magic doesn't need to be in this one." the irony—as i snapped their shot, the white fluffy puffball barking next to me was named magic!

so now, 48 hours shy of handing this text off to the lovely woman who is helping me bring the book to life, i'd say yes —i've been reassured that there's a whole lot of WUSHU MOON MAGIC going on—if we choose to look!

a note about the moons:
this book is organized by moons. you'll find that the text is separated into four sections—the four lunar phases of the moon. first-quarter moon is undoubtedly the longest—like most journey's, the most arduous. yet the last phase—the full moon—is the shortest, only one page in length. simple though most significant. new moon and third-quarter moon are sandwiched in between.

the book is also divided by moons of varying image sizes. 'mega-moon' images denote the four sections noted above; 'medium-moons' signify chapters; 'mini-moons' represent subchapters. my hope is that this schema helps keep the text fluid yet coherent—just as fiction is, supposedly.

so without further adieu, a little wushu from me to you...

## acknowledgements

special thanks go to the folks at the watson foundation. without your gracious fellowship in 2002, the essence of this story would not exist

additional shout-outs go to...

my grandparents:
grandpa, for your plentiful wisdom encouragement and insight
grumpy, for your inspiration gusto giddy-up freewheeling style
nancy, for providing me with every opportunity we conjured together
gp, for opening my eyes to the moon and china...and for the cover shot too!

my mom for supporting my hands scribbling across the page

my dad for covering my tail with last month's rent so that i could continue to write

my sister, jen, you mean more to me than anyone on this planet. you know that. and i know that. hell or high water. that's that

jim and marilyn for letting me crash so that i could pull through

the friends who gave me a kick in the pants recently: helping me to see that being misunderstood by others is an opportunity to better understand yourself

the friends [and one cuz' in particular] who supported me while i wrestled my own ghosts. i have never been so vulnerable. i have never felt so grateful to have you in my life

suz, cc, and ec for listening to the tale when there was still a lot to be told

the one encouraging soul who laid eyes on this manuscript. well, the one soul i 'asked' anyway ;)

jamie and his friend anna for making the cider press during the final hours of my long slog to the finish. your building blocks inspired me to get after it and get it done

liz for your support from the moment i started talking wushu

thomas for sharing your take on 'life' last week

debbi for bringing home the bacon

FINALLY, to all my lanterns and ghosts. thank you for the stepping stones—igniting and inspiring me to leap forward—even when the moon is hard to see

*wushu moon magic*

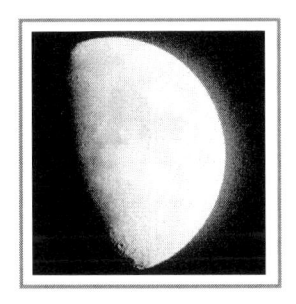

Between restless brushes with sleep, Byrd shifted in her rigid airplane seat and rubbed her cramped neck. She rolled over to face the window and eyed a ray of pastel blue light slipping its way through a sliver of space. She checked the time—7 am—and accepted four hours of sleep to be sufficient considering the turbulent flight. As the plane shot through the sky toward Vietnam, like a BB from a smoking gun, <u>D. Beak's words</u> frayed Byrd's nerves. *were frayed by —*

"Look Byrd, your photographs aren't cutting it anymore. They're stale. I'll fund you on one more field assignment. But heed this advice—take only two lenses, the ones already lodged in that head of yours. Find a new way by which to capture the essence of the human condition. If you see something new, I'll send you back to snap the shot. If not, I'm afraid I'll have to replace you. Byrd, you MUST find a fresh view!"

Byrd's peaked hands shimmied the cold plastic blind up its windowsill in trembles. Resting her clammy forehead against the frigid window, she peered out on a bruised black and blue sea swaddling an expansive dark green peninsula. With a drastic plunge in altitude, a creaky set of wheels punctured the engine's drone and Byrd's seat jostled like the pendulum of a finicky grand-father clock. She braced herself firmly against its back and muttered to herself under shallow breaths. *You can do this Byrd, just focus on the icicle.*

As seat trays rattled and babies wailed with the turbulence, Byrd closed her eyes and recalled a pleasant memory, her initial experience behind the camera lens at age eight. One sunny March morning in Vermont, she spotted a lone icicle hanging outside her bedroom window. Propped up on her bed, she kneeled transfixed and watched it melt—collecting in a pool of liquid at its pointy tip like a swollen teardrop. The drop welled until it burst then disappeared mid-flight into a pile of snow-coated ice.

Byrd vividly remembered darting to her dresser and fumbling hastily in the top drawer for the pink camera she received for Christmas fully loaded with a fresh roll of film. She snapped twelve shots and submitted the single image in focus to a magazine photography contest unbeknownst to her parents.

Three months later, Byrd found a green check in the mail made out to her in the amount of $100. Since then she figured that any image was worth the stubbed toe and missed school bus it took to capture the shot, and she would find a way to make ends-meet capturing what she saw. Many years later, as her Asia-bound plane descended in jolts and jerks upon a city wrapped in crystal glaze and morning haze, Byrd willed her eyes wide-open to find a fresh view.

When Byrd shuffled out of the airport terminal in a disoriented stupor, Ho Chi Minh City greeted her with an irksome onslaught of honking horns and sweltering heat.

"Where you want to go?" A sturdy cabby nudged her shoulder, his hefty hustle beating out his colleagues' slower steps.

"District 6 please." According to Byrd's guidebook, this neighborhood, better known as Backpacker's Haven, was the place from which all roads began in southern Vietnam. She planned to grab a quick bite to eat, scope out accommodation, set her compass to city bearings, and get to work.

The cabby led her to a maroon four-door, dropped her single piece of luggage—a worn red backpack—on the tarnished back seat, and showed her around to the other door. Inside, cool air conditioning and a radio broadcaster's tongue ruled her senses. The cabby squared himself off to the steering wheel and juiced the thirsty engine with his foot.

His delayed turn signal was met with abrasive honks from behind, though he brushed them off with a snarl through the crooked rearview mirror. He whipped the cab ninety degrees to the left, then chugged with traffic in a low gear toward a blossoming oasis of buildings in the distance.

Within the relatively nondescript miles to her destination, Byrd rummaged through her backpack searching for D. Beak's final set of vague though explicit instructions. She remembered reading the small handwritten note on the plane as it thundered down the runway departing New York City, but she couldn't recall where she'd stowed it thereafter.

She dug into the worn back pocket of the jeans she'd worn the previous day. No luck. She reached further into her backpack's depths and retrieved an inspirational note from a friend sealed in a plastic zip-lock bag. She unzipped the bag and fumbled with its contents. No instructions there either.

Byrd held her breath as she picked up a Vietnamese guidebook with several dog-eared pages. She propped the guidebook's spine up in her right palm and grazed its pages with her left hand. They splayed like a fish on a barbeque skewer then stuttered abruptly toward the back of the book. The note card fluttered haphazardly onto Byrd's lap. She sighed in deep relief then slouched back into her seat and devoured its contents.

在东南亚满足饥饿的鬼魂; 在胡志明市第六区,
在亚洲的会址招呼他们; 注意他们不会回应哀怜.

途径陆上; 然后在对最终城市的海岸下由海运,
在灯笼的为时; 获取饥饿的鬼魂并且显示什么您看见.

By the third read, Byrd felt she had a decent translation of D. Beak's puzzling poetics and scribbled an English rendition on the flip-side of the notecard.

*Meet the Hungry Ghosts in Southeast Asia;*
*In district six of Ho Chi Minh City,*
*Greet them at the Meeting Place of Asia;*
*Be aware they won't respond to pity.*
*The route will be overland;*
*Then down the coast to the final City by the Sea,*
*At the last of the red lanterns,*
*Capture the Hungry Ghosts and set them free.*

Byrd folded the card over in half, then hoisted her hips into the air, and stowed it in her back pocket. She let the specific clues of the assignment slip momentarily, and recalled her initial job interview with D. Beak.

"Byrd, do you know why I am going to hire you?" The masculine-looking woman wearing a wig to cover her bald head didn't look up from Byrd's CV as she spoke.

"I would presume it's because you think I'm a decent photographer, D. Beak." Byrd wrestled uncomfortably with her shoes beneath her seat as she sat facing her boss-to-be.

"Well, actually, it has nothing to do with your photographs. I see from your resume that you studied Chinese in school. I am passionate about Chinese poetry myself." D. Beak laid Byrd's CV on the table, rapping her fake fingernails shaped squarely at their tips on its glass surface.

"I believe that taking good photographs is a lot like reading Chinese poetry. Both are about learning how to interpret and share the world that we see. Look, I can tell you this, Byrd. The other candidates for this position are better photographers than you, but they don't speak Chinese."

Byrd was stunned by D. Beak's comment, but accepted that if speaking Chinese was what landed her the esteemed photography job she was after, she would take it! Meanwhile, D. Beak leaned back in her chair and eyed her new team member.

"Byrd, I can tell by the expression on your face that you are eager to have this job. But let me tell you something you should remember every time you head out into the field on assignment for me." Byrd recalled vividly that D. Beak then leaned forward across the table intently, so closely in fact that the garlic from her dinner the previous night was obviously apparent. She spoke in long slow semantics.

"Byrd, do you realize that the four lines of any Chinese poem have the capacity to render more meaning than a 300-page novel? Depending upon which way a Chinese poem is read—either left to right or bottom to top—the reader can arrive at a variety of conclusions." Byrd nodded, she had read enough Chinese poetry to understand the nature of D. Beak's comment.

She agreed that the Chinese written language was more symbolic, pictorial, and expressive than any Latin word derivation. Though still, Byrd was entirely uncertain where D. Beak was going with this claim, so she remained silent for her boss to continue.

"Byrd, the specifics of each assignment I give you will arrive via snail mail in the form of a poem. While I may not pen brilliant masterpieces like Wang Wei or Du Fu, the onus will be on you to extract the details of the assignment from the poem's schema. Do you see what I mean?"

D. Beak's final sentence echoed in Byrd's head as the cab belched and burped its way into the outer limits of Ho Chi Minh City. When it finally hiccuped at an intersection and the tired engine stalled, Byrd's focus snapped back to her present surroundings.

She watched the cabby turn the key over with a jerk and a cuss. The cab jumped forward nudging the car in front, and another angry horn beeped. A gangly cyclo driver peddled his way around the jam, up over a crumbling street corner and then bounded back down the other side.

Byrd jostled the window down its ruddy panel and leaned out as far as her seatbelt would allow. The sun blazed brightly on her forehead, and an intensified level of pressure collected in a strand of sweaty beads across the bridge of her nose. Depending upon the outcome of this assignment—*if she did not see what D. Beak meant*—it could be her last.

But before Byrd's mind leapt down that path, leaving a pile of strangled creativity and mangled focus in its wake, Byrd shoved Fear to the recesses of her mind and rolled up the window.

She glanced out the opposite side and watched Vietnamese school kids bounce down a cluttered sidewalk on colorful inflatable balls. A family of four sped down the main drag piled high on the banana seat of a red moped. As the cab idled, Byrd soaked up her initial impressions of the city like a dry sponge and summoned her strength. *I WILL find a fresh view. But first, I need a good meal and a bed!*

When congestion finally dissipated, the cab lurched down a buzzing tourist drag flanked by pastel pink and yellow buildings, each adorned with distinguished white trim. The French colonial edifices sat juxtaposed next to a string of squat ramshackle huts housing cafes, souvenir and Internet shops. Overeager signs hung from their rooftops beckoning to tourists, while shopkeepers buzzed around cranks raising their awnings for the day.

Under one particular awning, Byrd spotted a cafe adorned with lush fake plants and cozy yellow lighting. "Here, this is good, thank you." She paid the cabby in shiny purple dong, swung the squeaky door open, and hoisted her backpack onto her hips. She waved goodbye to the driver through the heavy air and scurried toward Lady Văn's Café.

Byrd took refuge from the sun at a small table under the red and white awning, offloaded her pack, and wedged it out of view under the table. A teenage boy with a wide smile and an overgrown bull-cut arrived promptly, and placed a glass of cold water on the plastic tablecloth. The cafe's decor struck Byrd as a hybrid between the little French bistro and seedy burger joint at home.

Before she had a chance to tuck in her chair, the waiter whipped out a menu from behind his back and presented it to her like a rare book. Byrd smiled politely at the boy as he backed a single step away from the table. She opened the menu, skimmed its surface, and was relieved to find that it was in English, as well as in Vietnamese and French. Byrd digested its offerings, and glanced uncomfortably at the boy's feet, still one step behind her shoulder. When he didn't move, she decided hastily on 'Option Number 33: Traveler's Delight,' whose caveat claimed to be 'Our five-star entree of choice!'

A hot body in a stiff chair, Byrd sat uncomfortably and waited for her meal to arrive. She wiped a white napkin across her brow, dabbed it in the water glass, and pressed the cool moist cloth against the nape of her neck. She closed her eyes, tuning into the 1980s western music emanating from speakers balanced in the branches of a plastic plant. Byrd felt the gentle breeze of a fan blowing cool air from the same direction though she wished its gusts were stronger.

When Byrd opened her eyes again, she saw a woman wearing faux black leather pants, bangle bracelets on her left arm, and a black pendant necklace chatting with weary patrons at a neighboring table. As the woman leaned over the table to clear it, her necklace dipped seductively into her gold shirt. She retrieved it with a sheepish smile. Except for her decayed yellowing teeth, all traces of her third-world upbringing were concealed.

The woman appeared to be making her rounds, and arrived at Byrd's table in short order. She held out a delicate though steady hand and flashed a wide grin introducing herself as Owner Lady Văn. Clearly she ran her establishment with hospitality and a captivating smile.

"Pleasure, Lady Văn. Call me Byrd." Lady Văn offered a kind chortle.

"Byrd? Is that a nickname?"

"Yes, a friend gave it to me." Byrd replied with a return smile at Văn.

"Oh, I nearly forgot your meal!" Văn remembered when her hand holding the lunch plate like an hors d'oeuvres platter grew tired. Văn presented the dish to Byrd, rotating it a touch clockwise and then back a tad counterclockwise.

A scant few pieces of meat, some braised onions thrown on a bed of weak lettuce, and three tough-skinned potatoes stared up at Byrd. She masked her disappointment in a prompt reply, "Wow, how delightful—this Traveler's Delight!"

Văn countered with "Bon appétit!" an indication that French influence stood the test of time in the Asian city.

Yet when Văn was at safe distance, Byrd foraged mercilessly through the food for flavor and hid all extraneous evidence in the paper napkin folded in her lap. She didn't notice the discreet footsteps of the waiter creep up behind her and was startled when he whispered in her ear, "You like?"

"It's fine, thank you," Byrd stammered through a cheeky grin.

"Not my favorite either." The waiter scowled in bitter recollection of his own taste-test and stuck out his tongue. He gestured nonchalantly at the napkin on her lap, then back to the plate, suggesting Byrd place her evidence there for him to discard. The young boy drew his finger to his lips then smiled devilishly. *It was their little secret!* Byrd winked then sunk into her seat, a trifle embarrassed that she'd been caught.

The waiter cleared her setting promptly and returned with a complimentary Vietnamese coffee—a rich and flavorful counterpart to the dull meal. Byrd sipped the sweet melody of condensed milk and strong local beans buzzing with caffeine. Her lips lingered around the weak straw as nearby chairs emptied to a lull in lunch traffic.

Finally Văn returned to the table with the check and a mint wrapped in shiny green and red paper. "Byrd, I noticed you came in with your luggage. Do you have a place to stay?"

"No, not yet," a slight pause and sip of coffee, "would you have a suggestion?"

"In fact, my family operates small guest houses two blocks from here. I can show you if you like. We accept either long term or short term guests—whatever suits your needs." Byrd had read in her guidebook that this type of arrangement was customary—many small guesthouse owners also ran cafes, which they used as a means to become acquainted with prospective guests.

Though Byrd was slightly skeptical of this smart marketing strategy, she recognized that it suited her needs too. Plus she took to Văn's charismatic personality, so she nodded, "Yes, I would like to see what you have available. When would you have time to show me, Văn?"

"I can show you now." Văn set her note pad down and ferreted under the table for the pack. She heaved it onto a chair, then shimmied it up her tiny back before Byrd could recant.

"Oh no, that's not necessary, Văn. Please, I can carry that. It's awfully heavy."

"You guest in my country. I come to your country, you carry my pack. And I got many shoes! You will have very sore back." She cackled at her own joke and lurched toward the kitchen under its girth.

Văn led Byrd through a maelstrom of kitchen chaos—blazing woks sizzling with oil, chef's knives jabbing at wilted greens, and a stray chicken squawking under the sink. They made their way to a nondescript door graffiti-marked by black rubber shoe scuffs at its base. Văn jolted it with a bump from her backside, and the door flew open into a dingy and putrid smelling alley.

The women tiptoed through the filth in open-toed sandals, sidestepping deteriorated pushcart parts and heaps of banana peals before arriving at another makeshift door made of cheap wood—though this one featured a brass lock and latch.

Văn retrieved a key from her pocket and jimmied it until its teeth aligned with the hole's wards. The door released on its hinges and slid over a shiny foyer covered in spotless white tiles—an immaculate masterpiece signed by its craftsman with the faint circular strokes of a mop.

"That's my mother's handy-work," Văn acknowledged.

"She must mop daily to keep it clean," Byrd offered.

"Three times a day!" Văn stepped onto a bamboo mat inside the door, slipped her shoes off and wrestled her petite feet into a pair of snug slippers. She bent over a row wedged against the wall to select another pair for Byrd.

Văn swung around unsteadily to place them in front of Byrd's feet, yet overstuffed like a turtle unaware of its shell, she bumped into a red alter featuring a watermelon-sized Buddha. The round icon wobbled from knee to knee, though Văn steadied him just in time to preserve his seated fate. "Oh, that could have been bad!" she whispered to Byrd, eyeing the open door to her parents personal bedroom off the foyer.

Determined, Văn secured the pack on her back by a downward tug on sweat-stained shoulder straps, and checked to make sure Byrd was settled in her slippers. Byrd gave her a thumbs-up, so Văn lumbered precariously up the first concrete step of a hollow stairway. She found her footing and Byrd followed bracing the pack from behind. With laborious though in synch steps, the twosome huffed up three flights of stairs, stopping at each landing to rest and catch the breeze sifting through an open-air window.

Văn drew in a deep breath on the final landing, swung the door open, and swept her hand through the air. Breathless though slightly over-dramatic, she gasped "This...is...the...available...suite!"

Amused Byrd peered in on a simple and sparse room. Another pristine white floor, a double bed dressed in worn though clean sheets, and a simple card-table with a chair.

"It's nothing special, but cheap, bright, and clean." Văn dropped the bag on the floor and sauntered over to the window. She tugged the white curtain to the side allowing bright sunlight to filter into the room.

After a cursory inspection, Byrd turned to Văn. "I think this will work well!"

"Good, because I didn't want to carry your bag back down the stairs." Văn's candor and wit prevailed.

"What a great stroke of luck to meet you, Văn!" Byrd exclaimed both charmed and grateful.

"I'll let you get settled. You can find me at café if you need anything," Văn suggested in choppy though succinct English.

"Thank you Văn, I'll be by later today to drop off some money for rent." Byrd closed the door behind Văn's departing wave and collapsed onto the squishy bed.

During the first few moments of solitude in her new home, Byrd lay face-up on her bed studying water-stains on the ceiling. Her ears caught tacky western holiday carols slipping through the crack under the door from her neighbors below. She reached above her head for a switch on the wall to check the light and fan above—both functioned.

Byrd glanced into the bathroom, finding walls plagued by hideous mermaid tiles and a pink outdated toilet. Something seemed amiss, no shower? *There had to be a catch to such cheap accommodations!* She sat up and peeked around the corner to find a nozzle poking out shyly from the corner. The entire bathroom was a shower!

Byrd dropped her feet over the bed, stood up on weary stilts, and moved toward the open balcony. A black plastic box perched on the desk caught her attention. Her hand grazed its base for a dial but found a miniscule button instead. When she pushed it, a flurry of fuzzy black ants danced erratically on the twelve-inch screen to a racket of obnoxious cackles. Startled, Byrd jumped then poked the button with her pinkie.

She wiggled between the desk and the bed toward the balcony, then stepped gingerly into the sun avoiding a dead gecko on the concrete. Bending cautiously at the waist over the ledge, Byrd's head ricocheted like a fiery Ping-Pong ball following conical straw hats as they whizzed by on mopeds in both directions.

Finally a hunched-over elderly woman lugging two overstuffed fruit baskets on either side of a long bamboo pole broke the dizzying paddle game. One basket brimmed with miniature candy-sweet apple-bananas and brown dragon-eyed longans; the other was stuffed with a beautiful cactus-like pink fruit with tough leathery skin.

After a young boy on a moped clipped one basket and it swayed rambunctiously in circles, Granny stopped abruptly in the middle of the street to reposition the delicate tipping scale perched on her shoulder. After the basket's swaying settled, she continued up the street unfazed.

Next Byrd investigated the residential housing building on the other side of the thoroughfare. She spied a cluster of boisterous middle-aged men perched on barstools through an open third-story window. They puffed on cigarettes and slugged shots between ogles at a scantily clad blonde woman traipsing across a TV screen.

A stocky-framed woman dawdled into view, took a quick glance at the TV, then swatted the man closest to her with a grungy cleaning rag. The room erupted into masculine bellows, and the woman, clearly disgusted, stomped out of sight.

Reveling in her box-seat view, Byrd's senses gorged themselves on the tantalizing street feast. She gathered it all in with a fresh inhale and let it settle in her belly with a distended exhale. She arched her back fanning her arms up toward the sky, and grinned at the slight release in her chest as her breastbone readjusted in a comfortable crack.

She wandered back inside then took a long leap onto the bed, unintentionally sliding it a few inches to the right on wobbly wheels. She landed in a pile of rumpled sheets and sighed. Exhausted, Byrd slipped into a much-needed catnap.

Byrd shot up in bed when she woke to a thumping heart and cacophony of angst. She looked out the window at the sun to gauge the time. It hovered two inches above the balcony at approximately the same place in the sky when she looked at it last. She sighed, relieved that she hadn't been asleep for long.

*wushu moon magic*     25

Eager to get cracking on her assignment, Byrd straightened the bed sheets and drew them taut across the mattress, meanwhile trying to make sense of her assignment.

*Okay, I have to find the Hungry Ghosts and have no idea who or what they are. But typically D. Beak assigns me China-related projects. Perhaps this project is somehow connected to the overseas Chinese communities sprawling throughout Southeast Asia? That's a logical assumption, right? Since I am supposed to start here in Vietnam then travel to some Meeting Place in Asia and finally to some City by the Sea.*

Byrd thought about what she knew of the Chinese Diaspora from previous travels. She understood it to be a prominent entrepreneurial beast that wrapped its wings around the globe—leaving a trail of fortune cookies spilling off of restaurant buffets, Laundromats spinning in cycles, and pagodas wafting with incense in its wake. Her right brain relished the delectable smorgasbord of these images, while her left brain continued to analyze the assignment.

*Yet although the Chinese are a migratory clan—and dot nearly every major city on the map—they are fiercely loyal to their cultural roots. So much so that they typically remain connected by bus routes in foreign lands. So perhaps I can follow their overland trajectory—Chinatown to Chinatown—all the way to the City by the Sea?*

Byrd recalled the Chinatown buses that she'd often rode between Boston, NYC, and Washington, DC. They were cheaper than Greyhound, though typically slower, but were absolutely reliable for getting from one Chinatown to the next.

Byrd picked up the shabby pillow laying on the bed and plumped it with one final smack before drawing her hands to her hips. *Yes! I'll follow Chinatown bus routes to the City by the Sea!* Byrd's heart lifted as she raced down the stairs two steps at a time, hopeful that she'd pieced one clue of her assignment together.

But there was one thought that remained unresolved. With little indication as to who or what the Hungry Ghosts were, she wasn't precisely sure where to start.

Byrd stepped off the hotel landing and into a sunny street sweltering with oppressive heat. A dense plume of grey clouds collided with their puffy white cousins above. She hesitated for a moment then disregarded the urge to retrieve her rain jacket at the thought of three more flights of stairs. Instead she zigzagged up a congested walkway rife with pandemonium, darting around vendors selling sliced mango and juicy watermelon out of crude wooden carts.

At the street corner, she dodged a reckless teenage boy weaving his motorbike on and off the sidewalk. It seemed the 'walkway' was not quite a sidewalk after all—but a faded white line merely suggesting separation between foot and automotive traffic.

Finally Byrd shuffled around a family of six strung together with rigid arms like a stiff strand of pearls, and arrived in front of Văn's Café breathless. She waved to her new friend stationed behind the bar with an outstretched hand bearing a perspiring glass of cold water.

"Here, I saw you coming up the street."

"Thanks so much, Văn. The most expensive glass I will ever drink!" Byrd exchanged the water for a crinkled wad of sweaty dong for rent.

"You're welcome, Byrd. Thank you! What do you intend to do during your stay in Ho Chi Minh City?"

"Well, I need to find..." Byrd lingered on the last word. She hoped to have a more specific inkling of where to begin her assignment by the time she reached Văn's Café, but the street mayhem distracted her train of thought.

She prolonged her response with a long sip of water down to the bottom of her frosty glass, and replayed D. Beak's poem in her head scavenging its lines for clues. She reminded herself to try to see things from a new view.

*What if I read D. Beak's poem as if it's Chinese, from bottom to top rather than left to right? In that case, it might imply that my first clue is actually the last—a lantern. Perhaps then, that is where the assignment begins? And this would make sense, if this assignment does revolve around the overseas Chinese. What better symbol of a Chinatown than a shiny red lantern?*

Byrd noticed Văn's posture change, her restless hands perched on shifting hips, as she discreetly eyed her wristwatch. Byrd rectified that it was now or never, she'd have to take a gamble.

Byrd stuttered, "Can you tell me where I might find a red lantern?"

"That's easy, why didn't you say so? Just follow this rode all the way to the heart of Cho Lon." She stood back proudly, happy to be of assistance."

A slight smile spread across Byrd's lips. *Cho Lon meant 'large market' in Chinese. Of course, that makes sense! No one would deny that every Chinatown around the world is really one large market!* **Byrd was on track!**

Then Văn leaned toward Byrd and in a stealthy voice inquired suspiciously, "But why you want to go there? Cho Lon dirty. Not safe." Byrd wiped the smile from her face under the guise of a sweaty nose.

"I'm on a hunt for a...." Byrd stopped, "...for a lantern for my sister." Văn stared at her quizzically though nodded and pointed Byrd down the street. Early in her career, Byrd learned that it was essential to reserve the details of her assignment, even her profession, for a need-to-know basis. Ultimately any time she revealed the specifics, the people she met tended to behave differently—sometimes hamming up their actions through toothy grins, other times ranting, raving, or running away from the camera. Byrd sought their candid natural proclivities through her lens, so she kept her gig under tight wraps and simply glanced in the direction Văn pointed.

"Thanks Văn, you've been so helpful!" As Byrd turned back toward the hustling thoroughfare, she caught the first stealthy drops of an afternoon drizzle creeping out of the clouds. She stuck her palm out to catch a single drop when a hefty dozen fell.

The steady trickle gathered speed and intensity, and splattered in smacks against the ruddy pavement. Instantaneously dark puffy clouds filled to maximum capacity and burst into a torrential downpour. Byrd swiveled on her heels to catch Văn's eye.

"Monsoon season." Văn raised her hands to the sky in a nonchalant shrug. Byrd turned toward the street again, amazed.

Liquid partitions dropped from the sky in heavy blinding sheets. It reminded Byrd of the view from inside a vehicle at a car wash when a cadre of spray guns fire from above, enveloping the car in ripple after ripple of impenetrable water coats. She smiled at the thought and stared at the deluge rains of her first monsoon season. Though inside, she ached for her camera to capture one memorable shot.

Next she observed a crowd of tourists lined up in front of a wrinkly man under the awning of Văn's neighbors' shop. Byrd squinted to trace the vague details of his weathered profile while he held a barrel of plastic ponchos.

With a sudden stitch of gusto, Byrd darted the distance from Văn's awning to the souvenir shop. She smiled at the man and pointed to a dry poncho on top of his heap. He unwrapped the awkward garb from its package and helped Byrd slip her head and shoulders into its gaping pouch.

Byrd thanked him and started down the street, giggling at the touch of slippery plastic wedging between her legs. Locals peered out of covered doorways, pointing incredulously as she splashed through potholes turned to birdbaths. Rejuvenated by the playful newness of a fresh assignment in a foreign setting, Byrd tromped eagerly toward her first red lantern.

After two soggy miles sloshing down a motor-way turned water canal without a lantern in sight, Byrd's neck ached from its cranked position under her hooded poncho. Wisps of cold slick hair whipped her cheeks each time she lifted her head, so she kept her gaze down at her waterlogged feet in open-toed sandals.

Discouraged she ducked under the overhang of a leaky awning and peered through dingy windows into a tiny teahouse. A hot beverage appealed to her senses, so she turned the rusty doorknob and tramped across a tiled floor coated in a thick grimy layer of dust. No one in sight, she seated herself at a small street-side table sheltered from the elements by a stack of soggy newspapers jammed under the windowsill.

Byrd stared out on the dismal scene glumly when a teenage girl arrived at the table with a chipped porcelain pot steaming with hot tea. She sipped the strong green concoction, her eyes following loose leaves as they settled in the cup. Her gaze returned to the window and Byrd looked out on a hopeful turned dreary afternoon.

When the afternoon rain finally slowed to a drizzle, Byrd watched locals return to the saturated street. A little girl in a bright red jumpsuit emerged from a covered alley pushing a cart of candies up the street. Her forlorn eyes and pencil straight lips suggested she was tired of a long day's work. In her final sales pitch, she called out wistfully to potential customers.

✓An indescribable sadness burdened the weight in her cart and made Byrd uncomfortable, so she stared at her bare hands on the table. For so much of her life, the camera lens had been her gateway into people and places. Now without it, she was uncertain what to do with the image in front of her. Since she couldn't capture the girl's unknown angst with a lens and lock it down on paper, the image lingered in her mind, its emotion running rampant. Byrd squeezed her palms together until they turned white. Growing restless, she stood up and left limp dong on the table before walking out the front door.

She trudged home in the direction of District 6, discouraged but adamant to try to find a lantern tomorrow, when the little vendor called out again. Byrd stopped and cocked her head in the girl's direction. Her ear hovered in the silence until the call erupted again. "糖果待售！" [Tángguǒ xiāoshòu! Candy for sale!]

Byrd's ears registered the familiar tonal tongue. It rose up softly, hummed across sideways, dipped high

*wushu moon magic*

to low questioningly, and then dropped down sharply in a final yap—the four tones of Mandarin Chinese! It was distinct from the more nasal Vietnamese conversations she'd heard from her first step off the tarmac that morning. Byrd spun on her heels and hustled in long eager strides toward the girl.

"Excuse me, do you speak Chinese?" The little girl nodded. Encouraged, Byrd smiled, then bit her lip deliberating what to ask next. Byrd doubted that the girl would know anything about ghosts, but being Chinese, perhaps she would know where to find the lanterns of Cho Lon.

"Do you know if there are any lanterns around here?" The little girl pointed back toward the teahouse. Byrd lowered her head to the little girl's level and followed her delicate finger to a lone lantern top, poking out above the teahouse awning from the street corner just beyond. Byrd realized she hadn't been able to see it through the rain. Relieved and reinvigorated, she thanked her little friend profusely.

She took a hasty step toward the red lantern, then hesitated and looked back at the girl. Though it seemed somewhat ridiculous to ask, "You haven't seen any Hungry Ghosts, have you?"

"No," the girl offered. Though after a long pause she added, "but Papa might be able to help you."
"Really?" Exalted, Byrd asked, "Can you take me to him?" The little girl lingered on one foot and kicked

the cart with the other. She twisted her head and looked up at Byrd through big eyes, "Yup, follow me!" she offered with a playful smile.

The little vendor swiveled the cart around in a looping semicircle and slid over to make space for Byrd at its helm. Byrd placed her hands on the rickety cart's handle bar next to her new friend.

As they stepped in sync, Byrd felt the little girl's gaze roll up and down the length of her body, studying her tan legs swinging out from a floral skirt and long hair draped in loose moist tendrils down the back of a lavender shirt. As the twosome pushed the cart with crisscrossed arms up the street, the little vendor's candies bounced up and down excitedly in the glass case popping like stray Mexican jumping beans with each pothole dip. Byrd's journey to find the Hungry Ghost's had begun!

"How old are you, 朋友?" [péngyou, friend] Byrd looked down on the shiny white scalp of her little friend's head where her smooth hair parted from left to right.

"Eight." The girl replied nonchalantly without raising her gaze from the ground. She exaggerated her strides to keep her pace in sync with Byrd's.

"And you have a big job to sell all of this candy yourself."

"Yes, but I've been selling candy since I was six," the girl offered matter-of-factly. Finally, she raised her head and glanced up at Byrd with a proud smile.

Byrd smiled back then looked up the street when the girl pointed. The first red lantern hung from a tall bamboo rod staked into the street corner. Byrd lifted her poncho hood and looked ahead, delighted to find an entire row of red lanterns painting a trail down both sides of the street. The lanterns were paired with vertical green street signs, their raised angular characters stenciled in crisp bold lines. It was clear they had arrived to the heart of Cho Lon—Ho Chi Minh City's Chinatown!

As they walked further down the street, Byrd's eyes lingered into long narrow shop stalls. She spotted floors piled high with medicinal herbs—dried mushrooms, bug carcasses, and seeds spilling out of cardboard boxes onto the floor in miniature heaps. The next stall sold Chinese decorations. Euphemisms written on lucky red paper dangled from a long white string over a table covered in colorful trinkets.

This stall was followed by another featuring specialty clothing. A plethora of embroidered garments, sheets, and pillowcases were tacked on display walls from floor to ceiling. Besides the obvious sellable goods' stalls overseen by aggressive shopkeepers, random restaurants and laundry shops crept into view, each bustling with an industrious Chinese spirit.

Finally, the little vendor veered the cart toward a bustling commercial center with an open-air market. They entered an aisle showcasing boxes of eggs stacked in orderly pyramids. It smelled rank of expired fish sauce.

They maneuvered their way through the aisle diligently, though a woman with an overstuffed bag of bean sprouts and green shoots scurried in front of them. She dawdled at each vendor stand to collect produce for a sizzling dinner stir-fry. Finally the twosome sidestepped her painstakingly slow steps and bee-lined through the rest of the market frenzy to arrive at an open street on the other side.

After they cleared a small crowd of congested shoppers, Byrd spun around and saw street lanterns spanning in all directions—north, south, east, and west. She grinned to herself. *No ghosts yet, but plenty of lanterns!*

Byrd's vendor friend directed the cart toward a sidewalk and stopped at the corner of a crumbling edifice. She tied the front of the cart to a cement block protruding from the building, while Byrd stared through a cracked window bursting with red paper lanterns. There were also bundles of incense sticks, stacks of red envelopes, and a collection of traditional Chinese instruments scattered in the bay window.

"Dad, someone here to see you!" The girl leaned back on her heels as she heaved the box of candy from her cart and placed it on the ground.

"Who is it, 妹妹?" [mèimei] Byrd recognized the familiar term, a common nickname for the youngest sister of any Chinese family.

"外国人." [wàiguórén] She chirped to relay to her dad that it was a 'foreigner.' A stubby round man in a thin white shirt stepped out of the dark room and into the doorway. He squinted at the light pouring through widening pockets in the clouds, then looked at Byrd with his hand over his brow.

Byrd cleared her throat and smiled uncomfortably. "Sir, I'm sorry to interrupt you, but I met your daughter on the street selling candy today." Byrd faltered, "I realize this might seem a bit odd, but I am looking for the Hungry Ghosts and your daughter thought that, well, that you might be able to point me in the right direction."

The man eyed Byrd suspiciously and crossed his arms, "They won't arrive for a few more weeks." Though it was neither the most receptive nor the most helpful response, Byrd was relieved to learn that at least this man knew of the ghosts.

He leaned against the door jam and cocked his head toward Byrd, "Where are you from?"

"America."

"What is your name?"

"Byrd, sir."

"And you speak 中华 [Chinese], Byrd?"

"Yes, sir. I studied Mandarin Chinese in school." The man finished wiping his greasy hands on a greasier apron and gave Byrd another quick one-up.

"Why you want to find the Hungry Ghosts?" Byrd thought about how to respond. *When in doubt, leave the answer simple.*

"I suppose I'm curiously amused by them, sir." She offered a pleasant smile, meanwhile wringing her hands uncomfortably behind her back.

"Curiously amused. Huh! Well, if you are still curiously amused in two days, you can come back and visit me and my family as we prepare for their arrival." Then he added, "I like to visit with foreigners. Maybe you have brother who want to marry my daughter." He laughed gleefully. Byrd could tell instantly that the man was reserved but had a warm heart.

She was delighted with his offer and her mouth widened into a grateful grin, "Thank you, that would be very helpful, sir!"

He nodded and added, "Call me Mr. Zhan." The man stuck out his hand with a smile. Byrd accepted his firm shake as he continued, "If you have free time before then, you might wish to visit the Chua Quan Am Pagoda. That is where the ghosts will appear on the 15th day of the 7th lunar month—about one month from now." Mr. Zhan pulled out a piece of paper and blue pen from the breast pocket of his shirt and detailed a street address in steady sharp strokes. He handed the paper to Byrd.

"I will do that. Thank you so much!" Byrd shifted her weight from one leg to the other hastily to start the soggy walk home before Mr. Zhan could recant his kind invitation. Instead, he offered kindly,

"Wait, let my older daughter take you home. You look miserably wet."

"Oh no, Mr. Zhan, it's quite all right."

"No, I insist. Where are you staying? 姐姐 [jiějie, oldest sister], please come!" He summoned his oldest daughter over his shoulder.

Steady footsteps echoed through the obscure shop interior until a slender girl with ink black hair and short bangs bounded out of the dark and into the doorway, flashing a neon pink tee shirt tucked into snug jeans. The rubber of her matching pink sneakers suctioned her feet to the floor and she caught herself on the door jam before toppling into the street. The girl's cheeks flushed pink and she waved at Byrd, rigidly propping her upper arm up with her elbow on her bony hip like a jack-in-the-box doll.

"Lin Xiuzhan, please take our friend home." Mr. Zhan turned to Byrd, "Where are you staying again?"

"Hello, Lin Xiuzhan, I'm Byrd." Byrd greeted the girl with a warm grin. "District 6, but..."

"I drive you, no problem," Lin Xiuzhan offered proudly in broken English grabbing the keys to the family moped off of a rusty hook inside the door. Mr. Zhan nodded in consent and directed Byrd toward the bike on the sidewalk with a wiry index finger.

"See you in two days, Byrd. 很快再见." [yī huár jiàn, see you soon] His dialect was thick, yet it was discernible enough for her to comprehend.

"Great, thank you!" Byrd offered still slightly amazed at her good fortune. She watched Lin Xiuzhan unhitch the moped from the street post and unweave a metal chain through its wheels. Lin Xiuzhan dropped the chain in a coiled pile which clattered loudly on the cement. She hopped on the bike and rolled it forward clearing stray bike tools from its path with her feet. Lin Xiuzhan inserted the key into the ignition and patted the space in back of her motioning to Byrd, "Hop on!"

Byrd lifted one leg over the bike and placed her feet on its worn foot pads behind Lin Xiuzhan's. As the bike ambled over the curb and onto the street, she clutched the seat bar at the base of her spine firmly.

Lin Xiuzhan maneuvered her way in and out of cyclos, cabs, and pedestrians, once coming so close that Byrd winced when she felt a passerby's clothing whip her arm. Lin Xiuzhan turned over her shoulder, "You like ride?"

"Uh, yes!" Byrd's answer encouraged Lin Xiuzhan to speed faster down the main drag.

A thrilling breeze broke the oppressive heat. They passed the first red lantern, and zoomed back into the city proper where fruit stalls replaced bread vendors, tongues rolled more and barked less, and brooms, though ratty, swept streets clean. The subtle differences distinguished the thriving though comparably grimier Chinatown from its host city.

"That's my place," Byrd pointed toward the mini-hotel on the opposite side of the street as the building came into view. Lin Xiuzhan darted through a break in traffic, skidded sideways, and arrested the bike with her foot, lining it up parallel with the curb.

"Lin Xiuzhan, would you like to join me for some tea before you head home?" Lin Xiuzhan glanced around, discreetly scanning a gaggle of women selling cigarettes at the street corner. She offered a quick reply. "No, I need to get home." Though before leaving, she scribbled her phone number on a piece of bent cardboard and handed it to Byrd.

"Here, call me sometime and I will show you around the city if you like."

"I'd like that, Lin Xiuzhan. Thanks again for the ride." Byrd peeled herself off the vinyl seat and pulled her damp skirt away from her legs. Lin Xiuzhan was already midway through oncoming traffic when Byrd looked up and her high-pitched horn bleated goodbye like a dying goat.

Byrd rose early the following morning, showered in her shower-less yet shower-full bathroom, and found an open noodle stand offering traditional pho—Vietnamese rice-noodle soup laced with a variety of seasonings including chile pepper and lime rinds. It tasted as it looked—light and fresh and warmed her stomach. She sipped the clear broth hastily, bypassing most of the noodles, eager to start the long walk to the pagoda in Cho Lon before the sun hit the street.

By the time Byrd passed the teahouse, the steamy walkway nuked her rubber souls hot to the touch. Byrd sought shade under a sorry-looking tree and pulled out the address Mr. Zhan provided. *The pagoda has to be around here somewhere!* She paced back and forth along the street three times then returned to the slight refuge of the tree.

Byrd leaned against its slender trunk, which sighed under her weight. As it boughed further toward the ground, the lower angle revealed a new view for Byrd and she caught sight of an elaborately embellished roof peeking out between two modern buildings.

The pagoda appeared to be locked in the middle of the block, so Byrd plodded around it until she found a side street. She followed a labyrinth of mini streets, until finally, she arrived at obscure #12 Lao Tu Street where two stone dragons guarded Chua Quan Am Pagoda's gate.

She entered a volleyball-sized courtyard, simple and bare but for two little boys playing ball, a stark contrast to the elaborate pagoda rooftop above. Trimmed with mystical ceramic dragons crawling out of Chinese legends, the beasts rippled along the roof's edge and met in a dance at its pointy peaked corners.

Byrd skipped up two steps to a hallway and stared up at an ornate ceiling with decorative wooden panels. She passed through an auspicious red lacquer door leading to a main hall and wandered toward the altar at its center. It was adorned by conical incense votives and gold trays scattered with pink paper and red candles.

Byrd recognized the altar's centerpiece, the Holy Mother A-Pho, from an Asian art history schoolbook. Her eyes traced the icon's wooden frame gilded with gold curves, as a middle-aged man shuffled toward her in floppy shoes.

Byrd offered him a gentle hello in a hushed voice, "你好." [nǐhǎo] His ears shot up in surprise when she spoke Chinese, but he offered a nod in return.

"Do you work here?" Byrd asked and the man answered again in quick short nods, his head flickering like the fruit images of a slot machine.

The pagoda keeper tugged gently at her arm and led Byrd through a side door down a stone walkway covered with rough tufts of wilted grass. They slipped around another corner and entered a small garden garnished with nondescript browning shrubs and waterfall statues marked with chalky white lines where water once bubbled.

Byrd followed the man toward a tablet flanking the exterior wall of the pagoda, which detailed its construction. Byrd skimmed one line after the next, which revealed in eloquent rhetoric that the Fujian 'bang,' the Chinese term for an ethnic community, built the temple in 1816. Byrd nodded to thank the man for pointing it out.

"Hard to read, want to know more, I tell you." He offered and gestured toward a simple wooden bench.

"Thank you," she accepted as they walked toward the bench. "Sir, I came here because a man named Mr. Zhan mentioned that the Hungry Ghosts are due to arrive here in a few weeks. Is that true?"

"Ah yes, August 18th they come here this year—the day when gates of hell open and ghosts with thin throats will wander the streets looking for salvation." He groped his throat melodramatically and chuckled in slight shudders.

"I beg your pardon, sir. If you don't mind me asking, who are these ghosts?"

"They are apparitions, wandering souls, of course. Some ancestors, some forgotten dead, others with no home at all."

"Why do they come?"

"It's their free day to come back and roam the earth without suffering."

The details of the ghosts seemed incredulous, but Byrd continued to probe. "Well, what do they suffer from?"

"All sorts of maladies, misfortune, and bad luck—either that they have caused or that has fallen upon them. We Living prepare food, drink, and entertainment for them—all sorts of lavish offerings here at the Pagoda." Then the pagoda keeper glanced at Byrd solemnly, "Ghosts possess great powers of destruction. If we don't honor their powers and appease them, they might destroy us. You come to Pagoda that day, you will see it crowded with people praying and making offerings for ghosts. It is a good day to visit Pagoda—must come early though—very crowded. Full of life and death."

Engrossed in his explanation, Byrd barely noticed a well-dressed middle-aged woman with black-rimmed glasses and two gold necklaces directing a young man up the walkway. He wheeled a large cart with a stiff pig tethered to its base, its limbs jabbing the air.

"See, like that, Yu family wants to make early offering. That family very superstitious, and that family's ghost have big appetite! You come back and visit in one month—you'll see."

Two days later, Byrd returned to the Zhan family souvenir shop. Sans Mr. Zhan the family sat in a semicircle on the shop floor hovering over a hefty pile of thin square sheets of red paper. Lin Xiuzhan stood up to introduce Byrd to the rest of the Zhan family.

"Byrd, this is my mother." A petite woman with an adolescent figure, glossy meek eyes, and smooth straight hair stood up next to Lin Xiuzhan and nodded. "This is Xiao Tangxiong, my cousin who is really not my cousin. He's a neighbor, but he's always hanging around, so we call him 'Cousin.'"

Lin Xiuzhan ruffled Xiao Tangxiong's fuzzy hair, its floppy soft strands slipping easily through her fingers. The boy appeared to be about ten and was dressed in a blue tracksuit. He smiled at Byrd through a gaping toothy grin and waved hello, cocking his hand left to right from his wrist.

Lin Xiuzhan continued, "And you met my little sister. We all call her, Meimei." Byrd and Meimei exchanged familiar grins. "Hi Meimei, nice to see you again."

"May I ask what you are making?" Byrd inquired.

"Offerings for the Hungry Ghosts." Mrs. Zhan continued, "Lucky envelopes that will be filled with money to greet them upon their arrival." Byrd scanned the stacks of prepackaged envelopes and bundles of ancient gold coins lining the shop shelves above Mrs. Zhan's head.

"Are all of those for the ghosts?" She asked incredulously.

Mrs. Zhan followed Byrd's gaze. "Yes, and we still have more to make. Come, we should get busy." She sat down and looked up at Byrd who stood still. "Ghosts have all sorts of sinful bad habits." Mrs. Zhan winked, "We must do what we can to keep them happy so they don't cause more trouble."

"Come, sit next to me and I will show you how it's done," Mrs. Zhan suggested. Xiao Tangxiong slid closer to Meimei, and Byrd wedged herself between him and Mrs. Zhan. Mrs. Zhan carefully selected a piece of red paper from the middle of the stack like a Jenga piece, and placed it face-down between them on the floor.

"To make an envelope, all you have to do is fold each corner in on itself so that the points meet in the center." She picked up two opposing sides, aligned their tips in the air, and made a brisk sweep over the entire surface to flatten both creases. She continued with the other corners then whipped the sheet around, double creasing each side while twisting it under the pressure of her index finger at the center.

"We have an assembly line. Kids fold, I stamp." She lifted a hot wax seal hiding behind her knee and embossed the paper at its center where all the points met. Mrs. Zhan lifted the stamp and eyed her work. When the stamp dried, she stacked it to the side where hundreds of finished envelopes lay.

"You will get the hang of it," she offered. Byrd selected a piece of paper and meticulously folded it with four creases as the family watched her laborious efforts.

"Now just a few hundred to practice and you'll be as fast as us," Xiao Tangxiong chimed in.

In the ensuing three hours of tedious folding, the family watched an international beauty pageant unfold on TV. The noise reverberated through the room in jarring dramatic voices; a rowdy commentary between a man with a deep bellow and woman with a high-pitched twang. As paper envelopes mounted, so did the hype on TV. Finally the contest dwindled down to five contestants on a sultry stage in Puerto Rico.

"Is Puerto Rico in America?" Xiao Tangxiong turned to Byrd. Before she could answer, the three Zhan women erupted in excited cheers as contestants made their grand finale across the stage clad in bikinis.

At this Xiao Tangxiong promptly stood up in a fleet of whimsy, pranced in front of his audience wagging his rear, and blew Meimei an air kiss through fits of giggles. The girls rolled their eyes and peered around him at the TV. Miffed, Xiao Tangxiong stomped his feet in frustration and snickered at their inattentiveness.

Realizing a dramatic exit was his best recourse, he pranced to the kitchen door pausing briefly under a beaded partition. He plumed his chest out like a peacock, tossed his head into the air as a final bon voyage, then twirled around and waddled out of sight.

"Don't mind him, comic relief from tedious preparations," Mrs. Zhan suggested. Uninterested by his antics, Mrs. Zhan and the sisters returned diligently to the envelopes with their eyes glued to the TV.

They watched as the winner was revealed. A starlet from Russia was presented with a sparkling crown to match her glistening watery eyes.

Meimei and Lin Xiuzhan exchanged wistful eye contact and matching shoulder slumps. Lin Xiuzhan looked down at her pile of envelopes and lamented, "If I were a ghost and this were my stash, I would have my skin whitened and my eyes widened."

"And you'd get a breast implant," Xiao Tangxiong jibed her from the kitchen door. Mrs. Zhan shook her head with a sigh, embarrassed yet mildly amused by his audacity in front of their guest.

Meanwhile Byrd was saddened to hear that the girls wished for more western appearances. She found them both stunningly beautiful.

When the clock on the wall ticked nine loud tocks, Mrs. Zhan clapped her hands briskly and uttered "Okay, getting late. Time to stuff envelopes. Lin Xiuzhan, I'll prepare a snack, please retrieve the coins and tell Byrd what comes next."

The sisters fetched a pile of heavy mesh bags from under the table and swept the envelopes to the side. As they dumped the bags onto the floor, ancient gold coins clinked and clanked through the air bouncing off each other like tiddlywinks.

Lin Xiuzhan offered simple instructions for what came next, though clearly, she was uninterested in the monotonous preparations. "Put coins in envelope, lick, and seal." This seemed mindless enough, so the girls got to work, meanwhile chatting about the contestants on TV.

Mrs. Zhan returned to the room carrying a tray and placed it on the ground next to the coins. The Lipton Tea's yellow label was easy to spot, and Byrd salivated at the refreshing pitcher laden with sugar granules still swirling toward the bottom.

Xiao Tangxiong accompanied Mrs. Zhan with a large covered bowl and set it next to the coins. Clearly yummy treats had aroused his interest in his duties again. Meimei lifted the napkin from the bowl, revealing a heaping treasure chest of sliced watermelon, papaya, and a mysterious prickly green fruit. The Zhan sisters reached over each other snagging toothpicks from a small jar and poked at the fruit with swift jabs.

Byrd waited for a lull in activity around the bowl then selected a triangular piece of the unrecognizable fruit. She spun it around on the end of her toothpick, and eyed its white meaty underbelly speckled with small black seeds.

"Mangosteen," Mrs. Zhan nodded.

Just as the children polished off the fruit bowl, Mr. Zhan appeared for the first time carrying a platter of glutinous round balls.

"Hi Byrd, welcome back to our home," he greeted her with a nod. "Please enjoy some 面包 [bāozi, bread] for all of your hard work."

"Thanks, Mr. Zhan."

"It is nothing," he insisted. "This food is cheap," humbling his family in typical Chinese fashion. He set the red plastic platter on the table, then prodded a doughy ball onto a paper napkin with a toothpick and handed it to Byrd. The ball was steamed to an overcooked noodle-like consistency and oozed with sweet pastry filling on one end.

Byrd took a bite while he watched her reaction. "Delicious! Thank you!" Mr. Zhan accepted the compliment with a nod, sat back in his chair placing one hand on his knee and selected a ball for himself.

With a full mouth he mumbled, "So are you enjoying the ghost preparations, Byrd?

"Yes, I hope you aren't too bored." Mrs. Zhan added.

"No, not at all. It's just that..." she hesitated, "I'm not sure I understand who they are, really."

"In time, Byrd." Mr. Zhan offered then looked at his wife.

"Come back next week and help us prepare food and effigies to honor the ghost's arrival if you'd like," Mrs. Zhan added.

Meimei piped up, "Yes Byrd, come back next week. Much more fun!"

"Thank you, I'd like that." Byrd smiled, hopeful to get a better sense of the ghosts on a return visit.

When the last coin was stuffed in its final envelope, the Zhan sisters yawned in tandem. Lin Xiuzhan stood up, "Come on, Byrd. I'll take you home."

On the way home, Lin Xiuzhan insisted they stop for a dinner treat. She pulled into an alley and led Byrd through the backdoor of a little Vietnamese pancake shack. Lin Xiuzhan selected an open space at a long communal table, and shouted to a chef whose eyes flashed up from his hot wok in acknowledgment of her request. Within minutes, a dish of delicate, thin, and flat circular cakes folded in half like Western crepes arrived at the table.

"These are made with flour and fried in a pan with a healthy dose of fish oil. We locals love them!"

"What's inside?" Byrd slouched to peek into the steaming cake closest to her.

"This one has shrimp, mushrooms, onions, and scallions." Lin Xiuzhan served Byrd the pancake and waited for her response.

"Delicious! We have something similar at home but make it with eggs and call it a crepe."

"Good, I'm glad you like it!" Lin Xiuzhan folded a large piece over four times in a swift knitting motion with her chopsticks and jammed it into her mouth. The greasy pancake settled halfway down her throat before its doughy mass collided with a barrage of questions forcing their way up.

Byrd watched as Lin Xiuzhan chewed hastily, jostling food from one cheek to the other. After a hearty chomp she garbled, "Do you miss your family?" She gulped forward in a scooping gesture and swallowed again, "What is the U.S.A. like?" Lin Xiuzhan cleared her throat with a resounding grumble and asked, "How come your hair isn't blond like Madonna's?" Lin Xiuzhan set her chopsticks down on her plate and leaned back awaiting answers.

Byrd's mouth gaped open in amazement that Lin Xiuzhan had been able to spit all of that out amidst an enormous bite. She regained her composure and answered the questions slowly, crossing her legs under the table.

"Yes to question number one." Byrd took a sip of water. She set the glass back down on the uneven table, and thought about life in America versus what she had seen in Vietnam. "Different to question number two."

Byrd uncrossed her legs and then crossed them the other way, "Regarding hair, I don't dye it, not everyone has blond hair in the U.S.," Byrd sat back and smiled, satisfied that she'd remembered all the questions in the first place.

Lin Xiuzhan acknowledged her responses casually with another bite and garbled again, "I want to visit U.S.A. Love to travel, only been to Guangdong, China to visit our ancestors."

"What was it like, to visit your ancestors in China?"

"I didn't really want to go honestly."

"Why? Aren't you the least bit interested, I mean, since you have Chinese heritage?"

"Not really," Lin Xiuzhan's voice trailed off into the water glass perched on her lips.

Byrd changed the subject. "Lin Xiuzhan, where did you learn English? You speak well."

"At school. We must learn Vietnamese, Chinese, and English."

"All three?"

"Yes, all three. My dad tells me at one point when he was in school, he also had to learn his bang's regional dialect, but we don't have to do that anymore."

"What do you mean, his bang's dialect?"

"Well, we are from the Guangdong region of China, so when he was in school it was mandatory for him to keep up with that dialect too. But nowadays, Cho Lon is smaller, less people from different regions in China, so we only need to learn Mandarin Chinese. Everyone uses Mandarin to communicate these days."

"I see."

"What about your friends, do most of them speak Vietnamese or Chinese?"

"Most speak Vietnamese at school and Chinese at home."

"Lin Xiuzhan, can I ask you something? What do you know of the Hungry Ghosts?" Byrd stuttered, "I'm sorry, I didn't mean to change the subject so quickly, it's just that I'm really in a pinch to understand a little more about these ghosts. Do you have any thoughts?"

Lin Xiuzhan hesitated, cutting the last pancake into even portions then offered, "I really don't have much to offer, Byrd. We younger generations aren't as amused by them. It's only the older generations, well, and perhaps Meimei, who are interested. But she's too young to understand their incorrigible ways." She shoved the final piece of pancake into her mouth with an angry jab.

"What doesn't she understand, Lin Xiuzhan?"

"The ghosts! She thinks they are fun and exciting, but all she knows is that we prepare special food and offerings for them. She has no idea what trouble they have caused. But I," she stammered, "I have learned enough about them to know that I don't want to learn anymore!" Her answer revealed a twinge of disdain more than simple disinterest.

"Wow, I'm sorry to hear that." Uncertain whether to probe further about what trouble Lin Xiuzhan alluded to, Byrd decided to take another approach. "Lin Xiuzhan, can I tell you something?"

"Sure."

"I'm on an assignment and need to learn whatever I can about these ghosts—who they are, what they look like, where they come from. I realize you may not want to talk about them, but please, if there is anything you can do to clue me in, I would be eternally grateful."

Lin Xiuzhan thought about this for a moment. Well, really my father is your best bet," she looked away from the table and then gave Byrd a long stare.

"There is one other person I know who might be willing to talk to you about the ghosts."

"Who's that?"

"He is a friend who has a high-profile job in our community. I can't promise that he'll speak candidly about the ghosts, but he does know them well. I can arrange for you to chat with him if you think that would help."

"Yes, Lin Xiuzhan, that would help immensely. Thank you."

"I'll call him when I get home. Plan to meet him tomorrow morning at the New World Hotel Saigon. He frequents the restaurant there to meet with dignitaries from all over the world. Perhaps he can chat with you between meetings."

"Great, thank you." Byrd changed the subject satisfied to continue her assignment tomorrow. "In the meantime, Lin Xiuzhan, if you aren't interested in the ghosts, what are you interested in?"

Lin Xiuzhan mused for a moment staring up at the crumbling ceiling, then grabbed Byrd's hand. "Come on, I'll show you!"

Stuffed and exhausted though intrigued, Byrd followed Lin Xiuzhan through the crowded food stall. They collected the moped and their helmets from the alley, and took their place in the congested lanes of post-dinner traffic.

Idling and impatient, Lin Xiuzhan back-peddled toward the alley, circled the bike in a three-point turn, and slipped it up the dark tunnel. The hazy beam of the bike's front light illuminated shadows of hefty rats.

As they sped through the dark, Byrd stared up at their parallel trajectory through the sky above. Phosphorescent city lights made the hour deceptive, giving the appearance of a sun dropping to its final descent for the day though it was much later. When the alley ended abruptly and the light opened above, Lin Xiuzhan gunned the bike into a busy rotary with an obscure monument at its center.

She careened the bike one-hundred-eighty degrees around the circle at full tilt, before swiftly standing it upright in time to peel off on a moderately desolate stretch of road to the right. As Lin Xiuzhan gunned the engine down the long drag, Byrd spotted the moon waning toward its last quarter, carved out perfectly like half of a pie in the sky. Nestled between two lone stars competing with city lights, it's steady beam guided them toward a part of town Byrd hadn't visited yet, bustling with the fanfare of a brilliantly lit night fair.

They whizzed by an old carousel, its neon lights blinking haphazardly as it tracked through the sky. The electric energy of the fair buzzed in magical beats, pulsing through Byrd's fingers, landing in a steady rhythm on her thighs. For one romantic moment, Ho Chi Minh City struck Byrd as seductive and fantastical—worlds away from the sweltering city beckoning her to find its ghosts by day.

Within a mile, the neon street fair gave way to an open expanse of land, and they zipped under a tall canopy of trees in the dark. Sporadically placed spotlights illuminated sinewy shadows on the lawn of a city park. Byrd squinted at the details blurred by the moped's speedy pace when Lin Xiuzhan brought the bike to an abrupt halt. She pointed toward a lingering shadow lurking under a large palm frond.

Byrd waited restlessly for the shadow to move again, though it appeared to have disappeared around the tree. "What are we looking at?" Byrd whispered.

Lin Xiuzhan giggled under her breath and started the bike again.

Once they were secluded in the noise of the engine's purr, Byrd asked, "Lin Xiuzhan, was that one of them? One of the ghosts?"

"No Byrd," she laughed, "that was two lovers groping each other passionately in the park."

"I'm sorry?"

"I wanted to show you why I don't care for those Hungry Ghosts anymore."

"Why is that?" Byrd inquired intrigued, "I'm not sure I understand."

"My boyfriend is Vietnamese, Byrd. The ghosts are a residue of the past and it's time to move on, if you ask me. Though my parents don't see it that way. They want me to marry a Chinese man to keep our heritage alive. My heart tells me otherwise. I can't honor our ancestral ghosts and love freely at the same time, so I choose love." Lin Xiuzhan's answer was simple yet complete and rendered Byrd speechless.

They drove back toward the city lights in silence. When Lin Xiuzhan pulled up to the curb, Byrd noticed her wet cheeks, the dregs of sadness slipping off her chin and seeping into her cotton shirt.

Byrd gave Lin Xiuzhan a tender silent embrace and walked inside. She trudged up the stairs and flopped on her back. She fell asleep face-up with her flip-flops clinging precariously to her sweaty toes.

The following morning Byrd strolled determinedly toward the New World Hotel Saigon to meet Lin Xiuzhan's friend. She walked into the lobby where a man dressed in a dignified green uniform with a white badge and a Beijing accent approached her.

"Excuse me young lady, are you Byrd?"

"Yes."

"Hello, I'm Lin Xiuzhan's friend Qi Xiaofeng, a pleasure to meet you!" He extended his hand in a cordial though professional shake.

"How do you like your time in Ho Chi Minh City?" He escorted Byrd through the stark lobby and into an elegant though sparsely populated restaurant.

"So far, so good. It's a bit hectic, but I am finding my way around and have met some lovely people like the Zhan family. Speaking of, how do you know Lin Xiuzhan? I'm not sure she mentioned…"

"I met her about two years ago when I first arrived to Ho Chi Minh City from my home in Beijing. Let's see, I think it must have been at the pancake house where I went to eat on my first night."

"How ironic, that is where she took me last night!"

"I'm not surprised, you can't come to Ho Chi Minh City and escape without trying Vietnamese pancakes."

"I see." A slender waitress arrived to the table, and Qi Xiaofeng ordered two Vietnamese coffees.

"Will that do?" Qi Xiaofeng checked with Byrd to make sure the order sufficed.

"Yes, that's great," she leaned back, grateful he'd chosen something her taste buds enjoyed.

"Another Vietnamese staple," he smiled. "So Byrd, Lin Xiuzhan tells me you wish to learn about the Hungry Ghosts."

Byrd nodded politely. The waitress returned and Qi Xiaofeng nodded appreciatively when she set the coffees on the table. He sat up straight then rested his hands in a clasp around his coffee cup.

"Well, let me start at the beginning and tell you about the history of the Chinese here in Vietnam. That will help you to understand the ghosts."

Qi Xiaofeng took a long sip of coffee and returned to his confident posture to detail the initial movement of the Chinese into modern day Vietnam before the Han dynasty. By the time he reached a summation of the past thousand years, Byrd's eyes had glossed over.

"You see, at that point, Vietnam was simply another province of China, and the southern Chinese migrated to find opportunities in a land less dense than their own." He paused to draw an analogy, "Like your country moving west...we moved south."

Byrd slouched when Qi Xiaofeng moved onto more recent history. She never was a history buff and hoped he didn't noticed when she glanced at her watch under the table.

Regardless he continued, "Many Chinese continued to migrate south from China seeking maritime trade prospects like rice. For the most part, they prospered in Vietnam, but trouble began for the overseas Chinese when Vietnam divided in the 1950s between the North and South, and the Chinese were required to join Vietnam as national citizens to fight in the War.

"You see, this was complex because if they joined the southern forces to fight Communist Hanoi, they would be fighting against the political doctrines of the Motherland—their roots—since China was a northern ally."

"Why didn't they just join the North then?" Byrd asked attempting to keep up with his pontification.

"Well, many of the Chinese migrants who flocked to Ho Chi Minh City came because they didn't agree with Communism to begin with. They fled China seeking economic freedom. And after all, at that time, Ho Chi Minh City—Cho Lon in particular—was a money hungry beast in the middle of a socialist society.

Qi Xiaofeng progressed methodically and slowly, "Torn between a new home offering financial opportunity in southern Vietnam and ties to their original roots—the overseas Chinese felt the divide of Vietnam as much as any Vietnamese family would have felt if they had family living in both the North and the South. At least that's the best analogy I can draw. Sort of like what you call a Catch-22, I believe."

"Yes, that is a Catch-22." Byrd took a sip of her own coffee and bit her lip.

Byrd stared intently at Qi Xiaofeng. The history he relayed seemed complex yet his eyes revealed little emotive expression. Byrd shifted in her seat and raised her coffee to her lips while Qi Xiaofeng continued.

He drew in a deep breath and provided one final long-winded explication. "So as you might imagine, when the North gained power from the South in 1975, the Chinese felt the blow here in Ho Chi Minh City. Stripped of their money and land, they were forced to either adapt to new policies and start over in Vietnam under the Northern regime or move elsewhere. The world they had strived so hard to create in a new home was literally shattered. Some stayed, but Cho Lon's population dwindled."

Qi Xiaofeng reflected for a moment as his pupils slid into the right corners of his eyes. He turned his gaze to the table and continued, "Associations shut down, newspapers dropped. There was only one school left in Cho Lon by the time all was said and done, and it was taught in Vietnamese. As a result, there have been very few Chinese migrations to Vietnam in the past thirty years." Qi Xiaofeng sat back seemingly satisfied with his explanation.

Byrd opened her mouth, though she didn't know what to say. She hid behind her glass, attempting to make sense of his comments.

Qi Xiaofeng broke the silence, "It was a tense time with some horrific outcomes." He paused, "Byrd…"

Qi Xiaofeng started then stopped abruptly and looked down uncomfortably at his feet. He eyed the shiny badge on his coat, then finally glanced back at her through softer though hesitant eyes.

Byrd picked up the conversation when he remained quiet. "Do you think there is still hostility between the Chinese and the Vietnamese now?" She thought of Lin Xiuzhan's comment in the park.

"Not really. Perhaps some of the older people still harp back to history's lessons, but the younger generations have moved on. Nowadays, the two populations are economically equal and all are Vietnamese citizens abiding by the same laws."

Qi Xiaofeng straightened the lapels of his jacket and sat up at a ninety degree angle in his chair. "Maybe they still feel a sting in their hearts, but for all practical reasons, there isn't any problem between the two communities anymore."

Byrd stirred in her seat, "Qi Xiaofeng, thank you for your insight. It's very much appreciated and I have a better understanding of the overseas Chinese population here. However, with all due respect, I was really hoping that you might be able to elaborate on the Hungry Ghosts."

"Byrd, I gave you as much insight into the ghosts as I can." He looked toward the door awkwardly and waved to a gentleman who turned before Byrd saw his face.

Qi Xiaofeng stood abruptly, "I'm sorry, Byrd. That's all the time I have today. I'm running late, you'll have to excuse me." Qi Xiaofeng stood up and straightened his shirt flat against his chest for the third time. He offered a flighty smile and stuck out his hand then shuffled to the door.

Byrd watched him walk across the street and flash his badge at a stern security agent patrolling the entrance of a cement building. He lunged up the steps in three long strides and was gone.

Byrd's frustration grew with each moment she lingered in the remnants of their conversation at the table. She realized that Qi Xiaofeng didn't even have to meet her in the first place, but she was perplexed by his abstract reference to the ghosts. Plus, he cast a wide net over the history of Chinese migration to Vietnam—though the net had loopholes and snares to untangle. As well, Byrd still didn't know what specific horrific outcomes he referred to.

For the first time, Byrd was relieved she didn't have her camera, because as of yet, there was nothing to photograph. She stood up from the table and walked home disappointed.

When Byrd returned to join the Zhan's for ghost preparations the next week, she found Mrs. Zhan wrestling a bag of sugar with wet hands.

"Hi Byrd! We're pleased to have you. Go join Mr. Zhan and the kids in the back room to make effigies and then come help me in the kitchen."

Byrd followed muffled voices to a dank workroom suffocating under low ceilings and dim light. The two girls and Xiao Tangxiong stood around Mr. Zhan, who held an assemblage of Styrofoam pieces together with plastic toothpicks to make a doll. They stood around a table littered with art supplies; open scissors, pipe cleaners slathered in glue, and miscellaneous paper cutouts shaped into doll clothes.

"Ah Byrd, just in time! We are about to give our King Ghost a new wardrobe! Meimei, where is that shirt you made?" Meimei scoured the table and found an orange shirt she had cut out of paper doused in shimmering gold glitter. She handed it to Mr. Zhan who fastened it to the doll's cylindrical stubby torso.

"And Xiao Tangxiong, where's that headdress?" Xiao Tangxiong handed Mr. Zhan his creation, also cut from orange paper, upon which he had detailed fire-breathing birds. Mr. Zhan fastened it to the Styrofoam head.

The children's eyes brightened as Mr. Zhan painted the details of the King Ghost's face. He came to life with purple skin and swirling gold cheekbones, beady red eyes, and an ominous set of fanged teeth enveloping a bright red tongue.

"Xiao Tangxiong," Mr. Zhan turned to the boy, "we need a long robe made of the same design as the King Ghost's headdress. Do you think you can do that?" The boy nodded rapidly.

"And Meimei, I think our King Ghost needs orange flames on his tongue. See those pipe cleaner's over there?" She nodded and grabbed two from the table. "Coil them around your fingers to make loops and then we'll glue them onto his tongue." Meimei got to work as well.

Byrd eyed Lin Xiuzhan sitting in a corner chair watching the scene from a distance, so she grabbed a stool from the table to join her. Byrd placed a warm hand on Lin Xiuzhan's shoulder who offered her a halfhearted smile in return.

"Lin Xiuzhan, tell Byrd what we are making," Mr. Zhan tossed the doll toward Lin Xiuzhan playfully, and wiped the glue from his hands on his apron.

"Effigies for the ghosts." Lin Xiuzhan offered nonchalantly.

Mr. Zhan scowled in frustration at his daughter, beseeching her to show more enthusiasm.

Lin Xiuzhan continued in a monotonous drone. "First, we offer these effigies to the ghosts at our alter here at home, and then we bring them to the pagoda where a ritual takes place. A monk will anoint our inanimate King Ghost, smudge his face and body with vermillion ink, and then light him on fire. King Ghost is then free to eat like a gluttonous pig." Lin Xiuzhan rolled her eyes while Xiao Tangxiong oinked in the background, much to the amusement of Meimei who giggled profusely.

Mr. Zhan continued with more spirited interest. "The rituals and offerings used to take place over the course of an entire month. Yet now it all takes place on a single evening here in Cho Lon. In cities with a larger, more prominent Chinese presence, the ghosts also reappear precisely one month following their initial arrival to earth as well."

Before Byrd could ask where these other Hungry Ghost celebrations might be, Meimei approached her father with a small paper boat in her hands.

"Papa, what do we do with this?"

Mr. Zhan looked at Meimei then at Byrd. "Well, that is also an effigy, Meimei. Boats honor journeys of all of our ancestors—their valiant efforts to reach new lands and painful demise when they crash upon the shores. He set the boat back down on the table and turned hastily toward Byrd, "We must offer this effigy for our ancestors every chance we get."

"Come Byrd," he tapped her shoulder, "let's see what Mrs. Zhan is making in the kitchen, shall we?"

Mrs. Zhan stood hunched over the countertop scrubbing feverishly at a stubborn black spot, and was startled when Mr. Zhan and Byrd walked in. "You two are just in time to help me with this batch of steamed fortune buns." She pointed toward a mixing bowl then turned to Mr. Zhan. "Any leftovers the ghosts don't eat will go to you!" She poked him playfully in the stomach.

*wushu moon magic*

"Yes, remember, I like mine with extra oil!" he cajoled her.

Mrs. Zhan turned to Byrd to explain, "What the ghosts don't eat, the clan members of our bang certainly will! I still think that's one reason we are so involved with the ghost rituals at the pagoda. Mr. Zhan loves these buns!"

"Come, wash your hands and we'll begin." Byrd rinsed her hands in a red plastic bowl on the counter, while Mrs. Zhan caught her up on details of the recipe.

"First I combined sugar and warm water, then stirred in yeast and let the mixture ferment a bit until it was light and frothy. Then I boiled the mixture until the sugar dissolved." She gestured again at the bowl on the counter.

"Now we'll add flour to the mixture." Byrd dried her hands on her pants and steadied the flour bowl while Mrs. Zhan poured the sugar water into a hollowed-out hole in the batter.

"Now, use your hands and mash the mixture together." Byrd slid her hands into the warm slimy goo. "That's right, keep going," Mrs. Zhan encouraged.

With a lull in conversation, Byrd piped up. "Mr. and Mrs. Zhan, if you don't mind me asking, how did you two arrive in Ho Chi Minh City?" She was curious about the Zhan's Chinese heritage ever since her conversation with Lin Xiuzhan over pancakes.

Mrs. Zhan prepared a pot of tea while Mr. Zhan spoke. "Mrs. Zhan was four when her family came from Guangdong to start a copper, tin, and steel shop here. I was seven when my family moved from the same part of China, though our families didn't know each other on the mainland. And my father retained the business of his father and started an ornament and celebratory knickknack's shop, which is what you see here." He pointed to the shop room.

Byrd stopped mixing and turned to Mr. Zhan. "I'm sorry to interrupt Mr. Zhan, but I'm just trying to keep the details straight. You said your families are from Guangdong, though wasn't it a Fujianese pagoda you sent me to the other day?"

"Yes, but things are different now than they were when we arrived." He leaned on the counter. "When we arrived, there were many more Chinese—predominantly from Fujian and Guangdong. Though our numbers have dwindled, so we share community centers now, like the pagoda."

"Right." Byrd watched Mrs. Zhan select three teacups off of a cracked tray and recalled what Qi Xiaofeng had mentioned about a dwindling Chinese population in 1975 after the North overpowered the South.

When Byrd's hands ached from intense mixing, she stopped to watch Mrs. Zhan refill the teapot with hot water from a silver canister on the floor. Mrs. Zhan felt Byrd's gaze though she did not meet it. Instead, she eyed the mixing bowl fastidiously. "Is the flour smooth yet?"

"I think so."

Mrs. Zhan tested its consistency. "Perfect, you can stop." She retrieved another bowl filled with watery pink food coloring from the refrigerator and set it on the countertop. She took the flour bowl from Byrd's hands and scooped out a small piece of dough the size of an egg.

"Next we dip a ball like this," she held up her scoop, "and drop it into the coloring. Be sure to knead it all the way through until it is evenly colored. Then we set them here," she plunked the ball onto a discolored baking tray.

Byrd followed suit, rolling a clump of dough into a round ball and dipped it in the food coloring. The dough soaked up the coloring quickly and instantaneously turned a light shade of pink.

"With two of us, it will go by quickly," Mrs. Zhan slid over to roll the dough into balls, and then handed them to Byrd for dipping. Within minutes, they amassed half of the flour mixture into pink round balls.

"Great, now you can cover those that you've dipped with this cloth, and I'll cover these." Mrs. Zhan gestured to a tray speckled by an equal number of uncolored kneaded balls on the other side of the bowl.

When they finished, Mrs. Zhan turned to Byrd. "We have to wait about an hour for them to harden, so how about some tea? Go join Mr. Zhan in the shop, and I'll bring the tea in after it's steeped."

Byrd agreed to the suggestion and wandered into the shop room, where she found Mr. Zhan moving a pair of red plastic stools into the dull light percolating through the dusty shop window.

"Here Byrd," he motioned toward a stool in the middle, "please sit."

"So Byrd, what have you been up to since we saw you last week?"

"Well, quite a bit of walking, taste-testing local cuisine, and sight-seeing, really. I also visited Lin Xiuzhan's friend Qi Xiaofeng from the Chinese consulate. He provided me with a history lesson's worth of information about the Chinese population here in Vietnam.

"However, I have to tell you," she paused, recognizing the opening she needed to ferret for more clues on her elusive subjects, "I went to chat with him in hopes of gleaning a bit more insight into the Hungry Ghosts.

"Yet when I asked him specifically what he knew about them, he mentioned he had told me as much as he could about their presence in Cho Lon. This baffles me because he didn't mention them once. All he alluded to were some horrific outcomes the overseas Chinese faced as a result of the War. Yet I still have no idea who or what they are.

"At this point, the only clues I have to go on are brief comments from the pagoda keeper and actually, Lin Xiuzhan. The pagoda keeper alluded to the ghosts as wandering souls, while Lin Xiuzhan suggested the ghosts represented your familial ancestry. Perhaps you can fill in the blanks as I must be missing something."

"Byrd, I realize you are curious about the ghosts. Let me see what I can offer you for insight," though Mr. Zhan hesitated. "But first, can you tell me something? The first day we met, you said you were curious about these ghosts. I get the impression they are what brought you to Vietnam since you seem more interested in them than anything else. And yet you came seemingly knowing nothing about them. THAT, I find curious."

Byrd faltered, she wasn't prepared for his blunt question; and debated whether giving the full scope of her assignment was necessary. Yet she rectified that when she revealed that the ghosts were part of an 'assignment' to Lin Xiuzhan, the young Vietnamese-Chinese woman kindly introduced her to Qi Xiaofeng. So perhaps it *would* be helpful to speak candidly with Mr. Zhan about what actually brought her to Vietnam in the first place.

"Mr. Zhan, please allow me to be frank with you. I came in search of the ghosts as part of a photography assignment for work. I didn't mention this initially because I've found in the past that I capture the most authentic photographs when the subjects don't even know I am armed with my camera." She stumbled on her words embarrassed that she hadn't been more forthcoming about the nature of her assignment.

"My apologies if my reason for being here seemed deceptive, that wasn't my intention. But I must learn more about these Hungry Ghosts and find an intriguing way to photograph them." She faltered then added, "My job is on the line."

Byrd looked at Mr. Zhan, the first person she admitted her plight to. He saw the vulnerable sincerity in her gaze and nodded compassionately then offered a prompt response, "Yes, ghosts are rather elusive, but now I understand your gumption." He didn't question her further.

Instead Mr. Zhan cradled a small teacup with both hands in his lap and shifted in his seat to release his crossed legs to the floor. His feet rocked up and down like a seesaw from heel to toe as he thought, searching for a good starting point to provide his take on the ghosts.

"Let's go back to what happened here in Cho Lon in the years leading up to the War, shall we? Did Qi Xiaofeng mention that the overseas Chinese dominated rice trade south of Ho Chi Minh City and throughout the Mekong Delta until the War?"

"Well, yes. He suggested that the overseas Chinese thrived here—predominantly due to rice."

"Okay, good. Did Qi Xiaofeng mention anything about French reign before the War?"

Byrd sat up straight, her curiosity piqued slightly with a new detail. "No, not that I recall."

"Ah, here is a detail that will help you then. Before the War, the French government barred non-nationals from eleven trades in Vietnam as an effort to diffuse 'foreign control' of the economy. This included the overseas Chinese monopoly control of rice. However, this was a MAJOR mistake. The ruling French government didn't think their strategy through, because when the Chinese were barred from rice trade, they simply up and left their fields! As a result, within just a few days, enormous quantities of rice were left completely unattended.

Vietnam's mainstay, their most precious commodity went completely—well, how shall we say—to the *birds*." Mr. Zhan winked at Byrd, acknowledging her namesake, though he was entirely serious.

"And that's not all." He continued more grimly, "Within literally days, nearly one-sixth of all currency in Southern Vietnam was withdrawn from the banks by international investors—simply because there was no rice to trade."

"In months the currency dropped to a third of its value. Quickly the government came to see that a major overhaul was necessary to rejuvenate Vietnam's economic footing after such a brutal self-inflicted fall. The conclusion? Chinese investment." Mr. Zhan paused to catch his breathe and add a side-note.

"I should tell you Byrd, that while this situation was grim for many, there were those of us who benefited initially. My family, for instance—due to what happened next."

"What happened next?"

"Well, Vietnam and China created an agreement whereby those Chinese with vested interests in textile, iron, steel, and plastic industries would be welcomed to Vietnam as immigrants."

As an aside, Mr. Zhan added, "That's how my family arrived here."

"The intention with the agreement was that we would open thriving businesses here, with Chinese networks on the mainland to establish cross-country trade.

"The hope was that this arrangement would prove to be mutually beneficial to both Vietnam and China. And actually, the results were astonishing. You wouldn't believe it but in 1975, Cho Lon controlled 100% of South Vietnam's wholesale trade—averaging about 80% of the trade industry on the whole!"

Mr. Zhan sat back and folded his arms across his lap proudly. "Cho Lon belched and burped like a fiery lion!"

Byrd smiled, it was wonderful to see him so proud of his traditional culture's place in his new country's history.

Then Mr. Zhan continued on a more personal note. "But truthfully Byrd, it wasn't just the economy that bustled with energy here in Cho Lon. Not for me anyway." A wide smile spread across his face as he glanced at the kitchen door. Finally, he looked back at Byrd.

"There was also passion in my heart. 1975 was the year I married Mrs. Zhan. It was an incredible time for me—business booming and sweetheart by my side. Mrs. Zhan and I believed that a life of nothing but success and happiness had just begun. It seemed we had struck a great fortune to move to this new prosperous land. Little did we know..." Mr. Zhan shook his head as if he were still in a fragile state of disbelief.

"But then a few calamities happened that you probably know well from your own American history, Byrd." Mr. Zhan paused, hesitant with his words, and shifted his focus from Byrd's eyes to his feet.

"Please, Mr. Zhan, continue. I'd really like to hear your thoughts." It was the first time she had spoken to a Vietnamese resident about the Vietnam War before.

"As you know, Vietnam became the battleground for a very nasty duel between international superpowers. The Chinese and Soviet Communist allies helped Northern Vietnam to fight Southern Vietnam and its allies, like the U.S.A. And on April 30th Saigon finally fell into the hands of Hanoi's rule. Yet what you probably don't know is what happened that day in Cho Lon, Byrd.

"When the Communist forces entered our gates, they found our streets lined with thousands of Chinese national flags and portraits of Mao Zedong, the Communist leader of China.

Ironically, the Viet authorities believed these flags to be symbols of Chinese chauvinism rather than national Communist support, and demanded that they be taken down. In days, many of us were denied our livelihoods, lost our businesses, and were considered to be too bourgeoisie. Cho Lon fell—we all fell—into a restless and disillusioned slumber."

Mr. Zhan continued with an even more grim tone, his back slightly arched, and his eyes staring at Byrd intently.

"After the War—when Vietnam began to stand on its own two feet again—relations between Vietnam and China deteriorated. As friction grew to the brink of disaster, the Vietnamese governance lashed out ominously at our presence here. Byrd, I am not exaggerating when I tell you that it became nearly impossible to find a means by which to live, work, and eat."

Mr. Zhan paused with his hand breaking the stale air of the shop room. Impassioned, he shifted in his chair to gain leverage on the seat when Mrs. Zhan peered into the room.

"Come, Byrd. The dough is ready." Byrd looked at Mr. Zhan. He dropped his clenched fist, sealed his lips abruptly, and looked away with guilt. Byrd didn't know what to do. Divided between Mrs. Zhan's festive preparations and Mr. Zhan's harrowing tale, Byrd sat still.

"Go ahead, Byrd." Mr. Zhan responded and motioned for her to join Mrs. Zhan in the kitchen. Though when she stood in the doorway, he beckoned to her quietly.

"Byrd," Mr. Zhan whispered, "That was the first horrific outcome Qi Xiaofeng likely alluded to. I'll tell you about the second later. I promise."

Byrd smiled halfheartedly. "Thanks, Mr. Zhan. I'd appreciate it." Even if she hadn't seen a specter of a ghost, at least she'd begun to understand the intensity of Cho Lon's history.

Mrs. Zhan hovered over the clumpy balls spaced evenly apart on wax paper. She looked up to greet Byrd with a nod then promptly resumed where they left off with the recipe.

"Next we flatten the balls into leaf-shaped discs. Her torso hovered over the far left corner of the sheet, and with the back of her hand, she gave each ball a sharp forceful slap. Her slaps picked up speed and intensity until she hovered over the last ball, then resumed with the recipe in sparse detail.

"Place pink leaf over white leaf, press down. Turn over, press down." She picked two leaves up to demonstrate and arranged them on a clean tray.
"Pink leaf over white leaf, press down. Pink leaf over white leaf, press down. You see?" Byrd began in the same fashion though Mrs. Zhan barely took notice, intently focused on coating the leaves in a thick layer of oil herself.

Then Mrs. Zhan fired up a wok and dropped the leaves in one by one. She removed them just before they turned a golden brown; sizzling, hissing, and splattering oil drops on the countertop. Mrs. Zhan cranked the heat up a notch and methodically moved through the the rest of the buns on the tray.

"These won't be ready for a while, Byrd. You must be tired. Why don't I have Lin Xiuzhan drive you home and you can taste them another day?"

"Sure, Mrs. Zhan." Byrd was caught off-guard by the tone of Mrs. Zhan's brisk comment. She rinsed her hands and scanned the woman's face for clues as to the sudden conclusion of the evening. It appeared to strain under conflicting emotions—sadness, anger, guilt, fear—though it was unclear to Byrd which was strongest.

*Have I done something to offend her? Been too nosy about the family or pressed too much to learn about the ghosts from complete strangers?*

Byrd ambled into the shop and found Mr. Zhan just as she had left him; except that his teacup was now cold, his gaze lost out the window, and his arms folded stiffly across his lap. He watched a stray plastic bag caught in a mini cyclone thrashing on the sidewalk. Byrd hadn't noticed how quiet the room was without the noisy TV. Mr. Zhan looked up at Byrd from his chair.

"Come Byrd, let me walk you out." He closed the door behind her and they stood under a humming lamp on the quiet street.

"Byrd, Mrs. Zhan gets upset when all of this history comes up, so I'll tell you the remainder of the story but please don't mention it to her. She really doesn't like to talk about it."

Byrd nodded, "I'm sorry Mr. Zhan, I didn't realize."

"It's not your fault."

"Let me pick up where we left off. As I told you, things got really bad post-1975, particularly for us in 1979 when Mrs. Zhan and I were expecting Lin Xiuzhan. That summer our families felt the tension of the tumultuous streets and opted to leave. Every sibling, and both of our parents departed, hoping to make it to Malaysia. However, Mrs. Zhan was in bed rest, very ill with Lin Xiuzhan. She and I couldn't go with them but promised to meet them after she was born."

Mr. Zhan turned toward the street lamp and drew his arms across his chest to watch a cluster of moths swarm around its paling glow. Byrd looked up as well, and counted nineteen winged ghosts flying blindly in the dark encircling the light. Finally restless by their aimless tizzy, Mr. Zhan turned toward Byrd abruptly and continued.

"We never did meet up with our entire family, Byrd. We eventually received word that except for my brother and his oldest son, none of them had survived the journey. They made it to Malaysia but only because they escaped the police and fled overland."

Mr. Zhan paused and looked down, "My brother, with what he has seen, he would never come back to visit." Mr. Zhan shook his head and fought to swallow the growing lump in his throat. "He was so angry, embarrassed and ashamed at the curses this land had brought him and his family. I have seen him twice since, but he too, recently passed away."

"I'm so sorry Mr. Zhan. I didn't realize..."

Mr. Zhan continued lost in his own thoughts. He wiped his face and appeared exhausted. Byrd backed away from further questioning, it didn't seem appropriate to continue. She stared down at the ground.

"Byrd, I was thinking, the ghosts don't arrive for another week. We should arrange a trip to the Mekong Delta for you. I have close friends who live on a little island south of Soc Trang. On the way, you can visit the Floating Fruit Market—all tourists love the market—and I'd suggest you also stop in a town called Ha Tien on your return. Ghosts are never easy to spot, Byrd, but the Mekong will help you understand what you need to learn next."

"I'd like that Mr. Zhan."

"Good, I'll call the Lin's and tell them you'll be there in two days. They love visitors." Byrd smiled and thought about asking for a lift home as it was dark, but then imagined that fresh air and a long walk might clear her head.

Instead the long walk only brought more questions and growing frustration. *What kind of wild goose chase is this? Why won't anyone just tell me about the ghosts?* The discomfort rose in her stomach. *Okay, so I understand the tumultuous history, political strife and economic turmoil the overseas Chinese faced. But what does any of that have to do with a Hungry Ghost?*

Two days later Byrd lay on a hard yet comfortable guesthouse bed in Can Tho, a bustling hub in the middle of the Mekong Delta. Beat from the long bus ride, her eyes scanned the dismal room for color though only found diffused traces from earlier days. She rested her chin on her right shoulder as she stared at a wall covered with little children riding giraffes on faded paper. She noticed the subdued pink and blue hues of a floral pastel mattress bleeding through a thin white sheet below her arm. A white fan jostled above in questionable circles, a little too sporadic for her liking, but its moan suggested that there was still life at the outdated hotel.

Rowdy shrieks flew through the window, and a loud uproar broke out in the streets when a goal was scored in the soccer game below. Byrd lay belly-up reflecting on the day.

When she boarded the bus bound for the Mekong at dawn, her head spun with city sludge. Her alarm hadn't gone off, she rushed around the room in a stressed frenzy to collect her belongings and pulled clothes in from the line outside on the balcony. Finally when she hustled down the street, a lone cyclo driver offered to peddle her the rest of the way to the bus station.

Byrd arrived in time to meet the bus as it rolled out of the station, though she couldn't be choosy about a seat. She eyed a metal cage lodged in the aisle between four front seats and spotted the beak of a hefty chicken poking through its slats. Her newfound traveling companion squawked when darkness descended on his cage and Byrd plunked down on his roof.

Bald tires jumped in and out of potholes and a rusty muffler puffed black soot as the bus careened out of the city. Instantaneously, the dancers of an outdated Vietnamese music video gyrated in perplexing techno dance moves across four greasy TV screens hanging from the luggage rack above. Corresponding love lyrics of a sugarcoated pop song blared from speakers Jerry-rigged beneath the seats.

A young mother seated next to Byrd held an angry baby on her lap. The baby's father, seated next to his wife, glared at his writhing son impatiently. Embarrassed by the disgruntled stares of fellow travelers, he whopped the baby on his bare bum and pinched his chubby leg with a sharp tweak. When the baby wailed louder, Byrd winced and shuddered, then gave the father a cold stare. Unfortunately he didn't notice, distracted by a steady stream of rain trickling in the window.

A friendly woman in the second row passed Mama a sticky glutinous rice snack. The young woman fed it to her son, and the teething baby mellowed. Seconds later, contented by the tasty oral distraction, he arched his back to the sky and gazed upward placidly.

The baby caught Byrd's foreign eyes and they exchanged toothy grins. The mother looked on proudly, while the father leaned over his wife toward Byrd. He pointed to Byrd's wristwatch then at his son. Byrd scoffed at his audacity, shook her head in disgust, and offered in rebuke, 'Sorry.'

The bus lurched south pausing briefly at red posts along the roadside to make bus stops. At one particular post, a brave woman hiding under a conical hat lunged at the door of the bus. She eked a single muddy shoe onto its first step and wrapped a muscular hand around the door's rubber frame. Byrd peered at the woman in awe, clinging stubbornly to the side of the bus as the vehicle picked up speed.

The woman clanged on the window with a woven basket bearing packs of imitation Wrigley's and Juicy Fruit chewing gum. Finally the driver noticed her and slid the door open with a metal hand gear. The woman shuffled up the steps, shaking her head back and forth refusing to pay for the ride, and then continued to accost passengers with an aggressive sales-pitch from the front of the bus.

When no one seemed interested in her goods, she hollered in a gruff bark at the driver to let her out and lumbered down the steps. Byrd glanced quickly over her shoulder out the back window of the bus to catch the woman strolling in the other direction as if the incident had never occurred.

When the bus finally descended upon Byrd's lunch destination in the city of My Tho, an aggressive hoard of cabbies swarmed the bus vying for her fair. A kind elderly woman nudged her boney elbows through the mass, grabbed Byrd's hand and shooed the men out of her path. Free from their harassment on the other side of the street, the woman dropped

Byrd's hand and hustled out of sight. *Strange!* Byrd thought, though grateful for the woman's care.

She ambled down a tree-lined street toward an open-air café and ordered a boxed lunch of fried spring rolls. Walking away from the café toward a worn park bench, she peered into the white plastic bag and lifted the Styrofoam top. Three scrumptious crispy brown sticks lay side by side, thicker than those she was accustomed to at home. They were wrapped in mint accompanied by a plastic container of dark brown oily dipping sauce that drew saliva to her lips.

Byrd settled on a bench in the shadow of a Nila palm with her lunch resting in her cross-legged lap. She closed her eyes anticipating a delicious first bite and opened her salivating mouth when a finger tapped her shoulder.

"Excuse me. Where you from?" Byrd twisted as much as she could without spilling, and locked eyes with a petite middle-aged man in plain clothes. Byrd sighed, the spring roll dangling midway between her mouth and the container and offered, "America. You?"

"Here, of course. Though initially from China." Byrd's ears perked up, she set her dish to the side, and uncrossed her legs to the ground. The man circled around the bench and stood in front of her.

Byrd was famished, but was also intrigued by this man's background, so she asked, "Where in China?"

"From Guangdong. Came penniless as a teacher, still penniless, now come to park to meet English speaking friends." He offered a kind smile, though Byrd remained skeptical of his motives.

*Was he fishing for handouts or genuinely interested in conversation?* He picked up on her hesitation, "I come to practice my English."

"Well, you speak very well. Would you like to sit down?" She offered after he'd already edged her bag toward her thigh to make room to sit.

He pointed over his shoulder, "You know what that building is there?" He continued before Byrd could answer. "That is the oldest Hoi Quan, Chinese community hall my ancestors built." He stared proudly at its crumbling façade in the old Chinese quarter.

He continued, "Chinese refugees settled here first you know, fleeing Manchus centuries ago. Then French seized control of Delta in 1860s. Town changed so much, we lost face." He shook his head regretfully.

"Thank you for pointing the building out, sir. I'm actually quite interested in the Chinese community here in Vietnam." She turned to face him more directly. "What else can you tell me?" Byrd propped her left foot up on the bench, her right foot fixed to the ground.

"You want to know the truth?"

"Of course, I always want to know the truth!"

"Well then, the Chinese and Vietnamese don't trust each other." He shook his head again, this time in disgust and continued. "Chinese population got too powerful in Ho Chi Minh City, then we were forced to leave. Many of us, we move here to make money. No money anymore though. No chance for a teacher like me."

Saddened he dropped both feet to the ground and glanced at a kid playing with a big ball in the middle of the park. "Chinese society still float through Mekong canals though, just look for buildings like that," he pointed to the community hall again. "Our pagodas and halls are too beautiful to destroy."

Byrd nodded in agreement.
"You know biggest difference between Vietnamese and Chinese?" Before Byrd could respond he answered his own question. "Vietnamese spend their money on fun, the Chinese save it. We thrifty and smart. We be powerful again."

Byrd was uncertain how to respond but her stomach grumbled, so she thanked him for the conversation, and made her way back to the bus to eat her lunch on yet another uncomfortable seat.

The tiny old yellow bus to Can Tho was even more cramped than the prior ride. One Byrd, nineteen Vietnamese bodies, their luggage, sellable goods, and children stuffed into three narrow rows. The single redeeming quality of the ride was the tantalizing panorama unfolding out the window.

Luminous green rice-fields interspersed by flooded arroyos mimicked a patchwork quilt that was delicately embroidered with water buffalos pulling plows and ducks waddling in their midst. As the bus slid through the fields on a dusty road like a cumbersome needle through a quilt, the roadside morphed into a street market of rice and incense baking bone-dry in the sun.

Three hours later, the bus driver finally yelled 'Can Tho,' and Byrd stumbled out the door onto a little dead-end street. Her entire backside tingled from lack of circulation. She followed local passengers in stiff steps around the corner toward a ferry carrying other cars, mopeds, and people into town.

A friendly Vietnamese girl hiding under a straw hat approached Byrd before she boarded the ferry, and introduced herself as Ha. Ha spoke decent English, and offered to escort Byrd over the ferry on her moped and then into the center of Can Tho to find a hotel.

Normally Byrd would have enjoyed stretching her legs with a walk after such a journey, but she was whipped. Gratefully she slid onto the back of Ha's bike, her pack still on her back and hand still clenched tightly around her lunch bag.

Ha's uncle was the owner of a decent hotel and she even brought Byrd so far as the door to her room. Byrd thanked her, though exhausted barely offered a smile. She slipped off her shoes, bathed herself out of a red plastic cup, drank some hot water, and tumbled onto the hard yet comfortable guesthouse bed.

Now as she stared at the crumbling wallpaper stripped of color and listened to the soccer game below, Byrd was grateful to be horizontal and opted to stay that way for the rest of the evening. The ghosts could wait another day.

The following morning Byrd spotted Ha perched on her moped at the curb in fresh though wrinkly attire. Refreshed and eager to investigate the Floating Fruit Market, which Mr. Zhan mentioned was just south of Can Tho in Cai Rang, Byrd strolled over to her new friend.

"Where you want to go today, Ms. Byrd?" Ha offered with a toothy smile picking at one toe with her fingernail.

"Actually to the Floating Fruit Market, Ha. Do you know of any good guides?" Byrd winked, her playfulness recovered after a sound night's sleep.

"I guide you myself. Follow me!" Ha hopped off her bike, and shuffled through the dirt toward an alley. Byrd hustled to keep up behind.

Ha led her through the back of a water-banana market stall and then over a rambling plank spanning twenty feet into the water, where a wide-brimmed wooden sampan floated.

Ha tugged at a rope tied around a plank post and drew the boat close so that Byrd could jump in. She nestled into a comfy seat complete with two cushions—one propped up against the wooden seat to provide back support and one resting on the wooden slats.

Ha loosened the boat's noose and jumped in herself, her sturdy body making a splash, and started to row the boat through a murky deep harbor. The boat drifted past boat homes and a variety of factories before arriving at a series of large blue boats riddled with dings selling fruit, vegetables, and spices.

Produce hung on display from a flag on each boat. "Ms. Byrd, what you want to try?" Byrd scanned the produce on the cluster of boats in front of her. "How about pineapple?"

"You want pineapple, I get you pineapple." Ha glided the sampan inches from the pineapple vendor's boat, where a middle-aged woman squatted squarely under her boat's awning. The vendor sliced a small wedge with a dull blade, using her body weight to cut through the yellow flesh and handed it to Byrd. Byrd licked its wet smooth surface. It wasn't the best pineapple she'd ever tried, but the intriguing way by which it came into her hands—from a woman in a boat in the middle of the Mekong—delighted her.

As Ha and Byrd meandered through the little market aisles—row upon row of boats tied together—Ha revealed the overall trading routes of the Floating Fruit Market. "Produce come from southern Mekong in big boats to smaller boats like this one here in Cai Rang. These boats carry produce to the Can Tho market further north. From there, the produce retrieved by merchants with outposts in mainland Vietnam. That how you get those limes in Ho Chi Minh City!"

Ha smiled and pointed to a nearby boat deck, where a little boy of about four years struggled to lift a hefty bundle of citrus fruit. He wrapped himself around the bag like a monkey clinging to a tree and tugged his forty pounds worth, but the gigantic bag wouldn't budge.

"Come on, now I take you to new spot where bigger boats can't float," Ha suggested. She navigated the sampan out of the open waterway and into a grove of dense palm trees with textured trunks, arching over a smaller canal speckled with luscious green pond lilies. A single red wildflower broke the unicolor green tunnel.

For three hours, they loitered through little aquatic passageways, under log bridges, and cruised around cheerful kids playing games on the muddy banks. Soapy old men bathed, while soapier woman and teenage girls washed dishes and laundry on the canal banks. Nearly everyone they passed waved, ventured a hello, or smiled through kumquat-laden teeth.

Finally they came upon a small plank in the middle of the canal that led onto land. "Follow me," Ha suggested securing her hat with her hand as she jumped on terra firma.

A small worn path led to a remote village nestled in the dense foliage. "This is Sugarcane Island, you must try some juice!" Ha led Byrd to a stall managed by two teenage girls, which the guide acknowledged were her cousins. It seemed Ha was related to everyone in the Delta!

Ha's eager expression turned into a fearful frown when she spotted a boy that looked a bit disturbed standing near Byrd with a rock in his hand. Byrd swiveled and caught the rapid blinks of his eyes then turned to Ha. Ha motioned for her to move away and warned, "Watch out, he's crazy and sometimes throws rocks at visitors."

"Great," Byrd suggested sarcastically. "Perhaps I can try cane juice another day then." Then as if the scene were scripted, the little boy picked up a rock shaped like a razor-sharp stiletto heel, and lumbered toward Byrd. Ha yanked Byrd's hand and they bolted into the circus stalls of the market, hoping to ditch him in the meat isle. They lost him through the potato aisle instead and sprinted to the safety of the boat.

Byrd jumped back in the boat and Ha gave it a swift push, motioning for Byrd to paddle further up the canal while she returned to fetch their juice. Ha insisted the juice was worth the trouble, so Byrd idled along the water's edge to wait.

Meanwhile Byrd spotted the boy making his way out of the dense island foliage toward the canal bank. So she propelled the boat with quick churns into the middle of the canal.

Byrd spotted Ha running up the shoreline, while the boy took off his shirt prepping to plunge into the water. Byrd's heart raced and adrenaline buzzed through her fingertips. Her firm grasp on the wooden oars gave her splinters as she rowed away from him.

Finally at a safe distance in the middle of the canal, she looked back then stopped paddling when she noticed him drop the rock and retrieve an undershirt jammed in his back pocket. *He's just changing!*

When Byrd reached Ha further up the shore, she found her guide with sticky fingers clenched around two plastic bags. Clear sugar cane juice slopped around in the baggies and was sealed with a rubber band around a straw at the top. When Ha handed Byrd her drink, the juice spouted out of the straw like a whale's blowhole. Byrd held both bags while Ha rowed back into the middle of the canal. Safe again, Ha and Byrd's close encounter drew laughter until both women's sides hurt from deep bellows.

When they entered another series of small waterways, Ha pulled the boat close to the canal's edge, encouraging Byrd to hop out and take a peek through the trees. Byrd steadied herself in the boat and lunged at the bank.

Her fingers fumbled for a sturdy root to pull herself up. Finally she found one, and hoisted herself onto shore. She peered through the trees, and spotted a close-up of the patchwork quilt she'd seen from the bus—a green sea rippling with single blades of grass fanning each other in the sunshine. The arroyo was enclosed by dikes on the farthest side and three canals flanked by banana palms. Their fronds splayed out over the field shading its perimeter.

Byrd couldn't imagine a more beautiful view in the Delta. After a few deep breaths to soak it up, she turned back toward Ha and offered a simple, "Thanks."

She dropped back into the boat with a slight jump from the shore. "We can go now, I can't imagine there's anything better than that!" With that, Ha escorted Byrd back to Can Tho in time to catch the next bus to Soc Trang. It was time to meet the Zhan family friend's— the Lin's.

Byrd lingered into yet another sparse hotel lobby, though this one was adorned with faux wood paneling, a puffy pink couch and two folding chairs. She selected the rusty chair facing the window to wait for Mr. and Mrs. Lin and peered out on a divided Soc Trang. A large canal spanned the windowpane horizontally and bisected the town into disparate halves, each riverbank a distinct contrast to the other.
On the far side, small squat wooden shanty homes abutted the canal's steep eroded bank. They rose up in a low single story, some adorned with tiled roofing, others thatched. School children chased stray dogs and played tag in the narrow alleys. Fishing nets and tackle leaned on each doorway, suggesting aquatic nourishment to be a community staple; though dark windows obscured an actual view of life inside the homes.

Byrd's foreground view revealed a seemingly brighter tourist side of Soc Trang. She pressed her nose to the window pane and studied the details of a dragon arching itself off of a Chinese pagoda roof. Its elegant head poked out over the dusty street where a couple ambled by hand-in-hand below.

Byrd watched them walk past the window and then turn into the hotel doorway heading toward the reception desk sans luggage. They chatted briefly with the short woman behind the desk in Vietnamese, who pointed toward Byrd.

The Lin's walked into the lobby, smiled in recognition of their visitor, and greeted Byrd with a wave. Mr. Lin's warm hand met Byrd's in the center of the room and brief introductions were made. "We are pleased to have you visit us, Byrd."

"The pleasure is mine, Mr. and Mrs. Lin. The Zhan's are a lovely family, and I am grateful you have all been so hospitable to a complete stranger."

Mrs. Lin smiled, "It's nothing," she offered. 关系 [guānxi, reciprocity] was the norm for Chinese families. Byrd knew that if the Zhan's or Lin's ever made it to the U.S., that she would have the opportunity to return the kindness.

"You've come at a good time, Byrd. We are also awaiting the arrival of Mr. Lin's older sister from Taiwan. She married recently and will be bringing her new husband to the Mekong for their honeymoon. She arrived in Ho Chi Minh City last night, but her plane was delayed and she missed the last bus to Soc Trang. You will get to meet them too as they should be arriving any moment now."

Byrd felt uncomfortable, "I hope I'm not interrupting a family reunion. I wasn't aware that you already had family coming. Are you sure I'm not intruding?"

"No, Byrd," Mr. Lin wrapped his hand around her shoulders. "We are happy to have you too."

"Mr. and Mrs. Lin, Mr. Zhan didn't have a chance to tell me how you all know each other," Byrd opened the conversation.

"Well, we lived in Ho Chi Minh City right next to the Zhan's once, but moved to Soc Trang in 1979. Actually Byrd, it wasn't where we intended to move, but it has worked out fine." Mr. Lin gave his wife a comforting smile. "When you come to our home, you will see we live on a lovely island amongst wonderful friends."

"Why does your sister live so far away in Taiwan?" Byrd asked.

"Our family is somewhat dispersed these days. She moved to Taiwan about the time we left Ho Chi Minh City, and we actually haven't seen her since. You will be a part of a very special family reunion today."

Mr. Lin turned to his wife again, "Why don't you take Byrd around Soc Trang and I'll wait for Jiejie?"

Again, Byrd recognized the familiar nickname for 'oldest sister.'

Mrs. Lin led Byrd across the street. "What would you like to see of Soc Trang, Byrd?" Byrd eyed the Chinese pagoda, acknowledging that it might be smart to see what she could learn about the overseas Chinese community here, though she didn't want to bore Mrs. Lin who had probably visited it a dozen times.

Instead she offered, "Take me to your favorite place, Mrs. Lin."

Mrs. Lin smiled and led Byrd down the street two blocks into an alley toward a small home with an open wall facing the street.

A middle-aged woman, her elderly mother, and two little children lounged on the floor of the open-air foyer, munching the dark green arrow-headed leaves of water spinach out of a pink plastic basket.

While Mrs. Lin exchanged a few words in Vietnamese with the middle-aged mother, Byrd smiled at the brother and sister. The woman smiled at Byrd, then pretended to hold a camera up to Byrd's face. *How odd, how would she know I am a photographer?*

Mrs. Lin grabbed Byrd's hand as the duo followed the woman to a dark room in the back of the home. When the woman flipped a light switch on the wall, they stood in the middle of a fantastically fun studio.

Two luminous spotlights stood in the center of the room next to three fairy-tale landscape backdrops. One depicted a western saloon, another a Chinese landscape painting, and the third, the gnarly craters of a moonscape.

A rack ran the entire length of another wall stuffed with costumes of all sorts and sizes: a sixties go-go suit, dragon costume, Buddha with a rubber belly, and an array of modern western dresses. There were also a few *daiyi*, traditional Chinese garbs like kimonos. It was an assortment of western style and eastern convention. As well, a plethora of high-heeled shoes sat like soldiers in a row underneath the rack.

Byrd smiled, the scene started to make sense. *So it was actually this woman who was the photographer!*

"Come Byrd, let's have our picture taken. My friend says we can pick out any costume we like."

Mrs. Lin perused the dresses until she found a costume she liked. She pulled it from the rack and rotated it on its hanger to show Byrd, who giggled.

"Good choice, Mrs. Lin." The white wedding dress was delicate though faded, featured thick material over the bust, and thin layers flouncing from the midline.

Byrd opted for something nontraditional and smiled when she spotted a large lion head hanging from the wall. She pointed to it and the photographer used a pole to draw it down from its hook.

Mrs. Lin translated the photographer's Vietnamese comment back into Chinese for Byrd. "Normally this costume is for two people, but since I already selected a costume, you can wear it yourself."

"Yes, I like this one." Byrd smiled at both women then marveled at a long multicolored cape, which the photographer withdrew from inside the mask.

"It comes with trousers too," the photographer offered. She held out a pair of yellow nylon pants, though Byrd's attention was fixed on the mask, so the photographer draped them over her shoulder.

Byrd held the lion's head squarely up to her own and gazed into its glass-ball eyes the size of candlepin bowling balls. The lion's white fur-lined brows curled toward his temples then swept up his deer-like ears. A pointy green nose jutted out six inches from his face. The lion's movable mouth could open to swallow Byrd's entire head, and the bottom jaw dropped down like a flap to reveal a circular row of painted white teeth and an engorged red tongue.

The photographer helped Byrd carry the costume toward a closet covered by a full-length curtain. "Here, dressing room," she offered in English. Clearly other tourists had made a pit-stop at her studio and she'd learned a few useful phrases.

Byrd entered the claustrophobic space with a dirty mirror perched in the corner and heaved the heavy mask over her head. It was hot inside—the mask had been cooking in the morning sun on the wall. Byrd secured her head snugly into a little helmet wired to the top of the lion's head, so that her bobbing movements would stir the lion to life.

Out of the corner of her eye, she spotted a lever and pulled it down. The lion's pink cloth lashes blinked. She peered through its eyes into the main room and saw that Mrs. Lin was already dressed in her costume, waiting patiently for Byrd to start the photo shoot.

Byrd slipped the trousers on over her own pants, nearly toppling over under the weight of the mask, then shuffled back into the room, much to the delight of the two women. They grabbed Byrd's hands and led her to one of two stools in front of the western saloon backdrop.

The photographer took a few moments to arrange Mrs. Lin and Byrd like a newlywed couple. Joined at the hips, arms linked, it was a ridiculous sight! The bride to be and her furry husband on vacation, honeymooning at a western saloon.

As the photographer stepped back to take a few shots, Byrd's eyes glittered with joy. *Here I am, in the middle of the Delta, dressed as a lion, searching for a ghost... I'm not sure these were the new lenses D. Beak expected me to find, but it certainly is a new view!* The moment of humor and lightness lifted Byrd amongst the gravity of the looming assignment.

By the time Mrs. Lin and Byrd returned to the hotel still chucking at the Polaroid in their hands, Mr. Lin's sister and her new husband had arrived from Ho Chi Minh City. Mr. Lin entertained the newlyweds with *ma zhong* in the hotel lobby, a game somewhat like a combination of western chess and checkers.

They were surrounded by the Lin's children—two boys and two girls—as well as Granny, who sat perched on the back of the couch. The casual manner of their interaction made it seem as if the older sister had never left, but a lingering awkwardness revealed unspoken detail.

After more small talk, the family marched in a lengthy procession to a big dock and hopped single file into a motorboat. In the midst of all the commotion, Byrd missed the details of their destination but followed the family nonetheless. With all passenger's aboard, the boat's rusty motor raced through the open waterway.

They tore through the murky water at a steady clip until another motorboat sped within six inches and doused the entire starboard side of boat. The new hubby, dressed in formal attire, who was seated on a wooden slat in back of Byrd shivered like a wet dog. Though it was Grandma who got soaked the most, she laughed gleefully at her new in-law's shocked expression. For Granny it was just another ride on the Delta.

When the family finally arrived on the other side of the waterway, they traded the motorboat for a fleet of smaller sampans. Mr. Lin hopped in one with his mother while Byrd rode with Mrs. Lin in the second boat.

"Where are we going Mrs. Lin?"

"Home, of course, to the island."

"What is the name of this island, Mrs. Lin? I'd like to find it on my map." Byrd pulled out a soggy tourist map she picked up at the hotel.

"No, it wouldn't be labeled on your tourist map. Actually, I don't think we've ever had a tourist visit the island," Mrs. Lin replied.

The family caravan continued up the waterway in the morning sunshine and then slipped up a small canal. This siphoned into an even smaller canal whose width was suitable for a single boat. The family floated through the narrow passageway then arrived at a dead-end with a small ladder leading out of the water.

"Are we here?" Byrd inquired.

"No Byrd. We have to buy provisions for dinner tonight." Mrs. Lin tied her sampan to a tree trunk and helped Byrd out. In turn, Byrd turned to help the others but they sat content in their boats. "Come with me Byrd, the others will wait here." Byrd followed Mrs. Lin up the bank.

They meandered through a tiny path cut through a palm forest. Yet the palms were so dense, Byrd couldn't make out where they were going. Yet amidst the sound of snapping twigs beneath her feet, she heard muffled chatter.

When Mrs. Lin swept a final frond from the path, the grove opened to a clearing where a dozen elderly woman sat on their haunches under conical hats at a makeshift market.

Baskets of clay, plastic, and wood were filled with a medley of fresh produce—red chili peppers, full vibrant heads of cauliflower, lettuce, and spinach, clusters of ripening green papaya, a triage of coconut species, and bundle upon bundle of flaky rice noodles.

An older woman stationed apart from the others offered slimy fish on baking trays, and an arms length from her, a younger woman sold household items from Soc Trang: bundles of toilet tissue, stacks of red plastic bowls, and packets of chopsticks.

Byrd couldn't believe the little oasis she happened upon! Mrs. Lin perused the market quickly, scurrying over to the fish woman first. Squishy Mekong River bottom feeders, an eel of sorts, and something that resembled a toothy catfish intrigued Mrs. Lin. Though finally she pointed to a wide-eyed fish with black speckled skin and turned to Byrd, "Ugly fish, but not bad tasting. You'll see." She turned to the vendor, "We'll take that one." The vendor weighed the fish on her scale then slipped it into a black plastic bag.

Next Mrs. Lin marched over to the woman selling greens. She gestured at a lush veggie with a thick cruciferous stalk, "These are the freshest, Mrs. Yang's husband harvested these from the Delta this morning." She smiled at Mrs. Yang as she bagged the water spinach.

Finally Mrs. Lin walked toward the woman sifting bags of rice with her ruddy hands. "Rice is a staple of our diet, and it's so much more flavorful here than anywhere else in the world. We will make rice porridge to compliment the fish."

"Sounds great, Mrs. Lin." Byrd juggled the fish and veggie bags in her arms while Mrs. Lin paid for the slender fine grains.

"I think that should do it," she gave the market a final glance, "Oh, one more thing!"

"Byrd, why don't you select the fowl. I'll take the rest of the provisions back to the boat and get us settled." Mrs. Lin eyed two caged roosters. "We have many people and need to prepare a grand feast." Byrd knew it would be impolite to decline, but was uncertain how she might get the live roosters back to the boat.

"Sure, Mrs. Lin..." Cautiously, she walked over to the woman sitting on a crate near the rooster cages.

Byrd pointed to the two plumpest roosters skeptically. She withdrew a crumpled wad of cash from her pant pocket, and watched the woman wrestle the roosters into a gaping black plastic bag. The woman lifted the bag as the roosters jabbed stretch marks in its sheen, and tethered it to Byrd's hand. She waddled back to the canal with the bag jostling between her legs.

Mr. Lin led the procession back out of the main canal and through a labyrinth of smaller ones until they arrived at a gated water passage—literally with a chain across its width.

Mr. Lin tossed the chain to the left bank, it wasn't locked, so Byrd wondered why it was there in the first place. On the other side of the 'gate,' they paddled the final fifty feet of untamed canal and then arrived to a grove with houses flanking the left bank. The canal appeared like a neighborhood street complete with miniature births for each family boat in front of prefabricated homes on the shore.

Mr. Lin pulled into the third birth, tied his boat to a deteriorating wooden post jutting out of a small dock, and helped his mother out. Mrs. Lin slid her boat alongside Mr. Lin's so that he could extend a hand to help Byrd out.

On land, he guided her into a large courtyard where two mangy mutts chased each other on the hot cement in front of their single story peach stucco home.

Byrd followed Mr. Lin into a lively living area bustling with cousins and neighbors. The room filled with Vietnamese and Chinese chatter as family and friends gathered around a TV set snacking on nuts and fruit. Plates and cups clattered chaotically while deafening music roared from a dance video on the screen.

Eventually it seemed the entire island had filtered through the front door; there was no room to move and the party trickled onto the back terrace. As the party swirled around her, Byrd scanned the room for small details to focus on, as she might have done with her camera. Two little boys played with a lone marble on the hollow floor under a table where some men smoked and others gnawed on toothpicks. Yet in the midst of it all, a little girl curled up on a blanket in front of the TV and slept through the ruckus.

Byrd watched Mr. Lin's older sister retrieve a video from her handbag and make her way toward the TV. She popped in a video of the recent marriage ceremony in Taiwan. It appeared that no one had been able to join for the real festivities, but the family delighted in the shaky home video now.

Glancing around the room again, Byrd found an elderly woman—perhaps another grandmother—who seemed out of context from the rest of the family hubbub. She sat in the corner distanced from the festive commotion, fixated on a steady stream of ants trickling away from a half-chewed piece of meat on the bed. Granny observed the ants carry food parcels single-file up and down the crinkled sheets as they filtered toward a tiny crack in the wall.

Byrd stood still in the doorway for the better part of a half hour amused by the commotion until Mrs. Lin returned to find her with roosters still in hand. Fortunately, the darkness of the bag had seduced the birds to sleep and the load was less burdensome to carry.

"Byrd, do you know how to prepare a rooster?"

"No, I don't think so."

"I will show you," Mrs. Lin led Byrd through the house and out a back door to the small cement terrace.

Byrd held the bag while Mrs. Lin dipped her hand in and pulled out the larger of the two birds. With a football player's hunched posture, Mrs. Lin swung the rooster over her head, slowly at first, and then gained momentum. She swung until its neck cracked and its body weight dropped. Masterfully, she jumped sideways and let it drop freely to the ground with her hands on her hips.

"Okay, now you try."

"No, Mrs. Lin, I can't."

"Sure, you can." Byrd realized Mrs. Lin wasn't going to let her off the hook, so she scooped her hand into the bag skeptically.

The bird nipped at her hand with a sharp beak as she wrestled to find its long neck. She pulled it out and spread her feet apart imitating Mrs. Lin's pose. Byrd swung the bird around her head by the neck until she heard a crack. She flinched when the rooster's weight landed on her shoulder. Startled Byrd shrugged it off skittishly, and the rooster dropped to the ground with a thud. Byrd smiled, slightly embarrassed, slightly unsettled.

Mr. Lin met her at the door and insisted she join him at the table while the women prepared food.

"Perhaps you'd like to sit for a bit, Byrd?"

Mr. Lin nudged Byrd toward the dining table packed with uncles, brothers, grandfathers, and sons. He handed her a cold Vietnamese beer in an opaque glass bottle, and interjected the cacophony of Vietnamese banter to translate a mundane conversation about the weather.

Content for a moment to simply observe and tune out the conversation she didn't understand anyway, Byrd nestled in her seat and looked out the window at clouds shaped like stick-people, promenading arm-in-arm across sky.

As afternoon transpired into evening, all the guests convened around the table on chairs, stools, and each other's laps to nibble off of a smattering array of courses Mrs. Lin served to her guests. When she served the rooster, Mrs. Lin winked at Byrd and raised a glass sitting idly on the table. Byrd smiled and raised her glass discreetly, recalling its slaughtering earlier in the day.

More glasses were raised as toasts were made to the newlyweds and hearty cheers erupted when the wedding ceremony video was replayed.

As Mrs. Lin cleared the red plastic plates from the table, a debate ensued in Vietnamese. Byrd had no idea what words were exchanged, but half the people filed out the door without saying goodbye and debirthed their boats. Finally, Mr. Lin stood and wiped his hands coated in poultry grease on a napkin.

"Since no one can talk to each other very well—half our friends speak Vietnamese and our new in-laws are more comfortable with Chinese—we will find a common language. Karaoke! Since the karaoke videos are in English you will lead us, Byrd." Byrd smiled uncertainly though Mr. Lin winked.

"First though, I'll show you the rest of the island on the way. Come!" Mr. Lin led Byrd out the back door and lugged a motorbike laying sideways onto its wheels. They lifted the bike down a rickety wooden staircase ending in a swampy swath of land and picked up a worn dirt path. In the obscure evening light, Byrd felt her way onto the seat and wrapped her arms around Mr. Lin's slender waist. They sped into the enchanting jungle in silence.

◐

Chasing the path up and over narrow bridges, Byrd and Mr. Lin half-tread half-sped through an oasis of glistening foliage. Byrd giggled in delight behind Mr. Lin as dewy palm fronds splashed her face with a refreshing mist. When the walkway was too narrow or muddy, they walked the bike along the cool damp earth lit by the rays of an arresting first quarter moon.
In what seemed like half an hour, they arrived at a bar perched on unstable stilts on the other side of the

island. The echoes of a decent electric guitar overshadowed horrible vocals as Mr. Lin led Byrd around a wooden plank-way toward the bar's landing deck.

Prepubescent boys filled small plastic blue and red kiddy chairs flanking a makeshift dance floor in the middle of the deck. The boy's older siblings jumped into manhood, offering up their best variations of Michael Jackson's 'moonwalk,' while female compatriots giggled bashfully from the sidelines.

As Byrd meandered through the scene, light raindrops fell and within moments, the outdoor crowd flocked to the door carrying their chairs overhead as shelter from the rain.

Safe inside Mr. Lin turned to Byrd though she couldn't discern what he was saying over the boisterous bar scene and rain drumming on the tin roof. He held up a finger, suggesting Byrd wait a moment while he scurried to the bar.

Byrd moved toward a nearby fish tank that glowed green with iridescent lighting. Shiny slithering eels and fish the size of rats swam in and out of algae-covered rocks. Next to the tank two fruit trees bearing orange gifts on their bottom twigs shook slightly with footsteps on the floor. A TV hanging above captured reflections of the café crowd and red lanterns swayed from the rafters to a love song radiating from speakers camouflaged against a bamboo matted roof.

Entranced by the scene, Byrd barely noticed Mr. Lin return with a coconut in hand. Its top had been cut off and a straw protruded from its fleshy depths. "Try this, it is a local specialty." Byrd accepted the fruit and sipped at its milky froth.

"It's very good, Mr. Lin, thanks!" Byrd yelled over the racket.

Mr. Lin tried in vain again to say something but his quiet voice was no match for the crowd. Byrd held her hands up to gesture that she didn't understand, so he led her toward a karaoke machine at one end of the bar.

Mr. Lin handed her a plastic binder with song selections and pointed to Byrd's mouth then back to the book. She laughed and shook her head. Mr. Lin nodded then laughed. Byrd sighed, it was a no-win situation.

Byrd flipped through the worn pages spotting some familiar tunes—*Edelweiss*, a medley of Madonna hits, *Thriller*, then finally she spotted a song she knew well —Simon and Garfunkel's *Bridge Over Troubled Water*.

Byrd pointed to her song choice and Mr. Lin nodded. He slipped four heavy coins into the karaoke machine and directed her to a small red stool. He handed her the microphone and rustled a snag lose in the long chord.

*I can't believe I am doing this...*

When music filtered out of the poor quality speakers above, Byrd drew in a deep breath. Her voice shook unsteadily with the first line. She lowered the microphone and cleared her throat discreetly, drawing in another deep breath with her hand on her inflating stomach. She cupped her ear and began the second line. It came out more clearly and with confident inflection. By the second stanza, Byrd felt more at ease and closed her eyes.

She knew the lyrics well enough to get lost in thought as she sang, recalling the first time she heard the song from the back seat of a cold car one winter night with a friend in college. Its sorrowful melody tugged at her soul during a particularly challenging semester—the type of semester or time in one's life when it is filled with loneliness more than anything else.

The lyrics inspired Byrd so much that the day after her friend introduced her to the bittersweet ballad, she bought the album herself and listened to it repetitively for days.

As she stood on the stage singing now, she was transported back into the cold car where she sat shivering as her friend read the album's insert aloud. It revealed that Paul Simon wrote the song in the summer of 1969 while Art Garfunkel was filming the movie 'Catch-22' in Europe. Byrd hadn't thought much about the irony of this statement until now.

But when Mr. Lin came over and asked her why she selected the song, Byrd's response revealed that the album insert still resonated with her.

"It's not until life seems like a bridge over troubled water that you find out who truly believes in you—loves you—supports you.

And yet if you don't know who those people are in your life, life will *always* be a bridge over troubled water.

Catch-22 is that really, the only thing that matters is that you believe in yourself enough to find the people who believe in you."

Mr. Lin looked at her quizzically, so Byrd continued, "Here Simon wrote the words, while Garfunkel filmed them." Mr. Lin smiled, though Byrd still wasn't entirely certain he knew what she meant. She stopped talking and looked away because she wasn't certain how to continue.

Yet truly there was so much more she yearned to say. Though she didn't know the full scope of the family reunion Mr. and Mrs. Lin had graciously allowed her to join, she saw it for what it was worth. A bittersweet occasion—both sadness and happiness mingling in the canals—with the older sister's return to Vietnam. Byrd wanted to tell Mr. Lin that she understood what it felt like to be close to someone yet distant at the same time.

She looked out the window into the rain and watched the older sister gazing into the canal wistfully from the porch. She wondered if Jiejie regretted that she had elected to start a life with someone else so far from home. For that matter, Byrd wondered why she didn't return home more often.

Abruptly though, Mr. Lin interrupted her musing. "It's getting late Byrd, perhaps I should bring you back to Soc Trang." Byrd stared at Mr. Lin's sister, still lost in thought on the banks of the Mekong, though nodded to Mr. Lin. She made her rounds to bid the family farewell then followed him to the boat bobbing in the canal's gentle ripples.

Mr. Lin untied the weathered boat while Byrd clambered into its hull. Before settling into the boat himself, Mr. Lin pulled a lantern out of a box in the stern and lit its wick with a match. "Here Byrd, hold this so I can navigate." Byrd lifted the lantern from the seat and draped it over the boat's starboard side. Its flickering glow caste elongated shadows on the rippling water.

Mr. Lin reversed the boat with gentle strokes, then swung it around to glide down the canal. As Byrd held the lantern for him to see, she was reminded of her assignment and the red lanterns inside the bar. "Mr. Lin, I noticed quite a few lanterns in the bar. Are the owners Chinese?"

"Yes, actually there are a number of Chinese living on the island. We are about 7% of the total population in Soc Trang. Used to be higher though…" He shook his head discouragingly. Mr. Lin's expression reminded Byrd of the teacher she'd met on the park bench in My Tho. She wanted to ask him why the Chinese population dwindled here too, but they arrived at the landing dock, and Mr. Lin gave her swift instructions to tie up the sampan while he retrieved the motorboat.

Once she was seated, Mr. Lin gunned the engine. The motorboat roared voraciously in the night air and ripped across the open waterway. Its wake sent ripples out in both directions until Mr. Lin cut the engine a few hundred yards from the shore.

Byrd turned to Mr. Lin in the silence. "Mr. Lin, about the Chinese in the Mekong. You mentioned the population used to be larger." She hesitated, "Can you tell me what happened? I'm sure Mr. Zhan mentioned I'm trying to find the Hungry Ghosts, and well, he sent me here to see you, suggesting I might be able to glean a little more about them in the Mekong."

Mr. Lin interrupted, "Yes Byrd, Mr. Zhan did mention your assignment. And you are on the right path to deduct that the population loss here has something to do with our ghosts." He looked down. "But look, Byrd, you are a photographer. You understand that an image has greater meaning if the artist truly has a sense of its subject. In that vein, I cannot tell you who the ghosts are, you have to find them for yourself." Mr. Lin dropped his hands in his lap and smiled meekly.

"Stay brave Byrd, you are on the right track."

Byrd realized she wouldn't be able to press him for any more details, so she collected her bag and shifted her weight from the seat to her stiff legs and stood.

"Where will you go now?" Mr. Lin inquired.
"Mr. Zhan suggested I go to Ha Tien." Byrd drew the strap of her bag over her neck and synched it snugly across her chest.

"Oh yes, the border trading town with Cambodia. He probably mentioned that it was a Chinese refugee who claimed that town for Vietnam long ago. Make sure you visit Chinese cemetery on hillside."

"No, actually Mr. Zhan didn't mentioned anything about the town. But thank you for the hint, Mr. Lin. I will check out the Chinese cemetery."

Byrd hopped out of the boat. "It's been such a pleasure to meet your family, Mr. Lin. Thank you for including me in your family's festivities. I promise to look you up next time I come back to the Delta. I'm not sure when that will be, but..." Byrd looked down bashfully, her formalities an obvious facade to the uncomfortable good-bye. So she stopped and simply smiled at him. Mr. Lin returned the gesture, waved, and started the engine.

Byrd greeted another bus at the station the next morning to travel to Ha Tien. This time though, she arrived early enough to get a real seat next to a puny little lady with bony shoulders and a coin-sized mole on her left cheek.

As the bus traversed the countryside, the chatty woman rested one feeble hand on the strap of Byrd's backpack and pointed out the window to various objects she thought might be of interest, like a small Viet boy who sold wooden back massage devices out of his wicker basket on the roadside.

When the woman finally hopped off the bus in Rach Gia, a prosperous little trading post with clean streets, a manicured lawn encircled by statues, and freshly painted stucco-building facades, Byrd was ready for a moment alone.

As the bus lurched out of Rach Gia, she slumped down in her seat and looked out the window at another endless green oasis colored by brown water buffalo, thatched homes, and white hats sheltering field workers from the bright sunshine. Byrd studied the conical hats, their shape matching the rounded mountains dotting the distance.

As the route opened toward the horizon, verdant fields gave way to rolling hills and a stunning coastline. A beautiful expansive grey sea unraveled in front of her. She could actually smell the salty ocean.

Finally the bus descended through the midday haze upon another lazy trading town. When it chugged into the Ha Tien bus station, Byrd jolted forward and hit her knees on the front seat.

As passengers shoved their way briskly toward the door, Byrd sat in her seat waiting for the mayhem to settle. Finally she reached into the overhead rack, grabbed her backpack, and shuffled off.

She followed the locals over a metal bridge resting on old war boats and walked down a dusty street past fishermen ravenously chomping dried shrimp for lunch.

As the locals dispersed toward their individual destinations, Byrd ducked into a hotel and asked the receptionist if he knew anything about the Chinese cemetery. The shy 15-year-old boy pointed out the window and steadied his finger halfway up the first of three hills back on the other side of the bridge. Byrd thanked him and tracked back over the bridge along a lonely dirt road until she found a small path leading up the hillside.

The path ended abruptly at a small though colorful pagoda leading into a nontraditional cemetery.

There, clustered on the hillside were atypical red, green, and yellow tombs capped with orange tips; decorated with swimming dragons, leaping tigers, and flying phoenixes.

At the far edge of the cemetery, Byrd found a sign in Chinese noting that the graves belonged to a Chinese family who ruled Ha Tien in the 18th century. The sign suggested that the largest tomb located furthest up the hillside, belonged to Mac Cuu, the Chinese refugee and adventurer who initially seized the town from Cambodian control in 1708. Below the formal notations, many visitors had left their thoughts on the signpost.

The one which stood out most was scribbled in thick Chinese strokes. 'Here was a man who came to this country as a refugee, seized a town for his new country, and yet some of his ancestors are still not welcome on this soil.'

Byrd scribbled the crude commentary in her journal then took a last glance around the cemetery. It was beautiful yet shamefully hidden on the hillside. She thought she had an inking of what that particular tourist had meant.

Byrd meandered back down the hillside and along the road paralleling the town's main canal then took a seat on a bench to watch two boys hovering over the side of an old boat. They sung in crackly pubescent voices while two other friends sat on the shoreline watching their splashes enviously.

A girl of their age rode by on her bicycle. When they called her name, she circled around to say hello. Free from their parents, the children chattered in playful flirtation for a moment before the girl rode off.

Byrd enjoyed the light youthfulness of her last few hours in the Delta. As she glanced at her wristwatch to determine how much time she had before boarding the night bus back to Ho Chi Minh City, a voice from behind her spoke up.

"Mind if I join you?" A slender woman with noticeably sunken eyes dropped onto the bench slats, her feet lifting a cloudy layer of dust from the ground.

Byrd turned toward the Vietnamese woman. "Your English is really good," Byrd offered surprised by her clean accent.

"Thanks, I'm from America." The woman smiled under closed eyelids.

"Oh, I'm sorry." Byrd was embarrassed to have presumed the woman was a local Vietnamese.

"It's okay, how could you know?" The woman's eyes remained closed though she spoke. "I'm a student at

UCLA and am here doing some research." She opened her eyes, blinked in the sunlight and continued.

"I've made a long overdue pit-stop to visit my relatives in Ha Tien. Though it's been exhausting. Just to get here, I had to take a flight to catch a bus to a boat to another bus to a moped...and I'll have to make the same trip all again to get home."

Byrd sat quietly as the woman shimmied herself up from her slouch on the bench. "If you don't have any plans, would you like to join me for dinner? I've been on a small boat with my family all day and it's been rough at sea, if you know what I mean. I could use a break."

"I'd love too," Byrd looked forward to some company and liked the woman's witty candor. It had been a while since she'd chatted with someone in English too.

"Good, come this way," the woman gestured over her shoulder then added, "I'm Vu."

"Nice to meet you Vu, I'm Byrd."

With that the duo stood and ambled in silence to a little café of the woman's choosing. They sat at a table on the outdoor pier above an unkempt beach littered with seaside trash.

"The tofu is decent here in the South, though not as good as up North. The South is better known for its rice, obviously." She pointed toward the rice-paddy fields on the outskirts of town.

"Yes," Byrd was surprised by the woman's chatty commentary for being so tired.

"Vu, how did your family end up in the U.S., if you don't mind me asking."

"They moved from Ho Chi Minh City to Ha Tien in 1975 then to the U.S. after that."

"Do you come back to Vietnam often?" Byrd made a quick scan of the menu waiting for the woman's reply. She'd decided to go with whatever Vu ordered, figuring she'd know what was best being somewhat local.

"Since my family moved, I've returned four or five times." Vu paused to review the menu herself. "Think I'll go with the local special," she decided after watching a waitress announce the dish she delivered to an adjacent table. Byrd lifted her chin to peer into the bowl's contents in which a green fish with its head fully intact and gorging eyes peered out of a clear broth.

*Scratch that, I'll go with bun cha.* It was a vegetable option which Byrd knew she liked and trusted.

Vu looked up from her menu, "What are you doing here, Byrd?"

At this point, it seemed foolish to get into the details of the Hungry Ghosts so she sidestepped the true nature of her mission entirely.

*[handwritten: who befriended who?]*

"I've befriended a Chinese family in Ho Chi Minh City. They suggested I come down to the Delta, so here I am." Byrd squirmed in her seat at the incomplete answer.

Vu offered a prompt acknowledgment. "My Vietnamese ancestors are actually of Chinese descent too. They lived in Cho Lon once. I assume that's where your Chinese friends live in Ho Chi Minh City?" Vu picked up the wooden chopsticks from her place setting and snapped them in half.

"Yes, exactly!" Byrd sat up in her seat.

"Do you ever return to China?" Byrd inquired trying to glean more information.

"No, my family has little connection to mainland China at this point." A waiter arrived as she finished her sentence, and she looked up at him to order.

Byrd observed Vu's shadow discreetly in the candlelight, wondering why the woman's family left Ho Chi Minh City in 1975 and then moved to the U.S. The date stuck out in her mind because it was the very same that both Qi Xiaofeng from the consulate and Mr. Zhan alluded to as times of great duress for the overseas Chinese.

After the waiter scurried toward the kitchen, Vu drew in a deep breath and settled into her seat, "Ah, smell that sea." Vu looked toward the ocean where heavy rain clouds made their way toward the coast. She sat quietly for some time before speaking again. Then abruptly, she turned to Byrd.

"You know what I realized returning to Vietnam for my anthropology research?" Vu leaned forward in her seat, fiddling with the rippling tablecloth fabric in her fingers.

"What's that, Vu?"

"Vietnam is just like the rest of Asia. It is a country trying to get back to its original essence as it plunges into the global market. Yet what I've resolved is that this essence is pretty much just 'Asian.' I really don't even know if there ever was any original Vietnamese essence because the country was settled so long ago by overseas migrants.

"I'm sure that sounds strange, but if you think about it, the country became 'Vietnamese' with the passing of time. Truly though, all of Asia has the same roots. We all have the same essence. Makes me wonder what all the fighting was for..."

Byrd was unprepared for the poignant academia of Vu's comment and had little to offer in response. Fortunately, the waiter arrived with their dishes, momentarily sidelining their conversation.

When he left, Byrd tried to reply, "I'm sorry, Vu, I think I follow you, but…"

Vu interrupted, "How's your meal?"

"Oh, good," Byrd answered unsteadily. It seemed Vu had offered her thoughts and that was where the conversation would end. They picked at their entrees and ate the remainder of the meal in silence.

As Byrd nibbled through the second half of her bun cha, a guest of wind blew up swiftly from the sea and the precariously strung outdoor lights flickered. Byrd set her chopsticks down on her plate and leaned back in her chair.

She watched the grisly sea lap at the shore in swelling waves, tossing small wooden fishing boats tied to the dock sideways. The beach was now partially illuminated by a pale moon, though it was luminescent enough to reflect the white bellies of the boats as they bounced off each other's rims.

Vu also set her chopsticks down and peered distantly at the sea. She walked to the railing, stepped onto its rusty base and peered over, studying the boats' shallow glowing hulls. When she turned back to the table, Byrd thought Vu's eyes looked sorrowful and glossy though the woman avoided eye contact.

Vu sat back down solemnly, slurped the second half of her soup noisily, then stood up abruptly.

*wushu moon magic*

"I'm sorry, I'm really tired, Byrd. I'm going to go now. It was nice to meet you. Safe travels." Byrd watched Vu wander away from the table in astonishment. How odd!

Byrd sat in the dark motionless for a moment then picked up her chopsticks. She coiled the white rice noodles around them and dipped them into a bowl of dark gooey sauce. The sweet-sour sauce coated her tongue, and she chewed slowly to let it seep into her taste buds. The sauce was a distinct sweet and sour, unlike anything she had tasted before—much like the Mekong overall.

The land was exquisitely beautiful yet captivatingly raw. She recalled the boisterous family reunion at the Zhan's and the troubled boy on Sugar Island. The littered shoreline of the canals and stunning green paddies. Even this random displaced woman, so lonely yet so beautiful in her disconcerting solitude, as she peered over the dock on the stormy night. Each image escaped like a bubble to the water's surface from a precious treasure chest buried deep in the murky Mekong.

Byrd relished the details as she finished her meal, yet still grappled with the motive behind Mr. Zhan's suggestion to journey to the Delta in the first place.

She'd been in Vietnam for nearly one month yet felt no closer to the ghosts than when she'd arrived. Ironically, all she felt was a hollow ache inside that she couldn't understand. She rose from the table and stood where Vu had been watching the storm roll in ominously.

Byrd watched the tide lure a crisp white wave away from the shoreline and draw the boats back into the sea as far as their weathered ropes would permit. The moonlight speckled on the glassy gritty wet sand and the waterline receded. With a defiant rip, waves lashed at the coast and heaved two boats out of the water completely. They collided in midair, the newer of the two gouging the older with a deep groove in its hull. The smack of wood against wood echoed from the sea up to the restaurant and all of its patrons turned in surprise. With a thud, both boats dropped back down into the water and the old one filled with water rapidly sinking. The rope securing it to the pier snapped and the boat dropped out of sight.

Byrd stepped back from the railing stunned. For some reason, the inanimate brutality of the scene riled her senses. She returned to the table, paid the check in haste and scrambled to the bus station under the weight of her worn pack. Perched on a hot motor, Byrd nodded in and out of sleepless fits through the night ride back to Ho Chi Minh City.

The following day Byrd greeted the Zhan family with eager hugs outside the Chua Quan Am Pagoda gate in anticipation for the Hungry Ghost Festival. She sneaked a peek through the entrance gates, and caught wafts of incense spiraling madly out of clay urns. Gray smoke danced like tiny minarets into an equally grey overcast sky.

A sea of destitute and homeless Chinese mulled about the courtyard hungrily eyeing a table piled high with 金 [jīn, money]. This money would be collected over the course of four days and then distributed to them in fair share. In the meantime, Cho Lon's homeless graciously accepted free bouquets of red joss sticks from monks in black robes.

Byrd followed the Zhan family through the courtyard, her hand clasped tightly around Mrs. Zhan's wrist as they slithered through small gaps in the dense crowd toward the front door. When they reached an impenetrable cluster of people, Byrd shimmied herself onto her tiptoes to see what they eyed.

With a slight break in the crowd, Byrd found an elaborate table offering. She salivated at the mounds of fruit—clusters of vibrant orange tangerines and green pears interspersed with bunches of petite apple bananas and furry brown longans. Miscellaneous beverages including Coke and a bottled white liquor tempted the ghosts who preferred drink.

When the woman in front of Byrd shifted left, she noticed several individual ceramic bowls brimming with green and orange stir-fried vegetables and white rice.

Mrs. Zhan tugged Byrd deeper into the crowd, eagerly parting two older ladies, then politely asked an older man to step aside for Byrd to see. Finally she saw what all the fuss was about.

An enormous origami horse constructed of multicolored rice paper rested his hooves in two meticulously arranged clumps of grass, each wrapped with silk ribbon, at the centerpiece. Pink paper money embellished in gold insignia, red candles righted in gold candelabras, and copper urns filled with red and yellow smoldering incense sticks filled the rest of the table.

On the floor below, large candelabras featured red candles with dragon profiles etched in gold relief. Byrd feasted on the scene through the hazy air, though with so much incense smoke she could hardly breathe. She rubbed her eyes which already stung.

Mrs. Zhan suggested they move to a small extra step at the base of a column toward the back of the pagoda. There, on the outskirts of the thick fragrant haze, Byrd took in the scene in its entirety. She watched the yellow tops of flaming red joss sticks dart forward and back as overseas Chinese families fanned them through the air.

Small offering tables stood in each corner of the pagoda hall featuring ghost effigies contributed by families. Byrd spotted the Zhan family's honorable King Ghost figurine on a table flanked by dragon fruit and bouquets of bright lively carnations. Next to the flowers, she found two platters of meticulously arranged florescent pink fortune buns, like those she had made with Mrs. Zhan weeks before. Byrd squeezed Mrs. Zhan's hand to get her attention and pointed. Mrs. Zhan nodded and smiled.

Just when Byrd thought her senses might burst from overload, music wafted down a hallway and into the main hall. A traditional Chinese drum beat solitarily to set a steady rhythm. After several counts, two brass symbols chimed, followed by a melodious xylophone-like instrument that rounded out the hollow spaces in between.

When the instruments reached a collective pause, a steady stream of black robed monks marched single file into the room. They stopped and stood in place, while a monk dressed in a saffron-colored robe with a red sash and an austere expression met them at the center altar. The distinguished monk initiated the ceremony with a deep bellowing chant.

He retrieved a red pretzel-shaped ornament from the main altar, lifted it above his head and then lit a candle to start the procession. Mrs. Zhan whispered into Byrd's ear, "First, he prays to main god."

The black monks followed his lead, and a gathering of head clansmen burning incense stepped into line as well. Byrd caught Mr. Zhan out of the corner of her eye. He fell in line behind the last robed monk and placed a wad of money on the main altar bowing swiftly toward its centerpiece.

"What is Mr. Zhan doing, Mrs. Zhan?"

"He is requesting salvation for our ghosts." Byrd studied the calm, reserved, and giving man before he turned to march outside. She thought she noticed a lone tear stream down his cheek, but the hazy smoke obscured her view. Mr. Zhan fell out of sight just as the head monk reentered the main hall through an adjacent doorway. The head monk ducked inside then skirted quickly through a side hall.

"Those are the ancestral rooms," Mrs. Zhan pointed toward the door he entered.

Byrd peered inside and noticed walls covered in pink and red rectangular paper covered in beautiful black calligraphy strokes. There were also spiral incense sticks hanging from the ceiling that coiled like snakes and burned from outside to inside toward the name card dangling in the center.

Mrs. Zhan whispered in Byrd's ear again. "Those hangings represent the names of 2,000 ghosts from our bang. Each year living relatives have the option to buy a flag for their ghosts. "We did," she pointed to a section of the wall covered in 'Zhan.'

She paused slightly then resumed, "Unfortunately this year, the number of purchased flags have dropped even though the ancestors now most definitely outnumber the living." Byrd listened intently while watching the monk wave his ornament over the walls in elaborate sweeping movements.

Mrs. Zhan squeezed Byrd's fingers. "This is the moment you've been waiting for Byrd, the ghosts are about to arrive! The head monk is saying that he will now renew the breath of life for all the ghosts and that they are free to roam the earth." The monk lit the first flag on the far wall. Byrd watched closely through the hazy incense, though the smoke stung her eyes to tears. She blinked successively.

The monk shuffled from the first swatch of yellow hanging from the rafters to the last at the other end of the room. By the time he ignited the last flag, the room was brimming with smoke. Byrd kept her irritated eyes fixated on the wall hangings swaying gently from a breeze blowing through the front door.

The monk turned to face the doorway where Byrd stood, she shifted her stance slightly to make room for him to pass. To her disbelief he shuffled out as casually as he entered. Byrd stood stunned. She assumed that there would be some tangible evidence of the ghosts, or at least some ritual fanfare to suggest that they had arrived. Instead, the side hall was filled with nothing but burning flags, smoke, and silence.

Perplexed Byrd watched the monk amble toward a small altar in the back of the pagoda where a single candle cast elongated shadows on a small paper boat. He waved his ornament over the boat in a long fluid stroke like an orchestra conductor, then stuck his wand vertically up in a sand-filled urn next to the altar.

Immediately the music stopped and the crowd dispersed like a fleet of scurrying mice, invading every crevice of the pagoda to find their ancestral flags and honor their familial ghosts.

Mrs. Zhan released Byrd's hand. "I must make my own offering now, Byrd." She too shuffled away to find her ancestor's flag on the wall in the side hall, leaving Byrd alone in the middle of the room.

Byrd meandered over to the lone boat altar. She noticed its origami folds were amazingly intricate; tiny round windows flanked the boat's bottom birth. Transfixed by the empty and colorless little holes, she gazed in on the lifeless scene inside the boat.

The pagoda was silent but for the shuffling of soft-soled feet on heavy tiles, until a raspy voice floated in from the meditation garden just outside the door. "Excuse me, sir?" Byrd recognized the first intelligible voice to perk her ears upon arriving in Ho Chi Minh City. This time though, Meimei's pitch was calm, more serene than her persistent sales call hawking candy in the street.

"Mister, do your ghosts not like the rain?"

A deep voice responded, "No, my dear, they do not."

"Why is that?"

"The monsoon's of this land caused my ghosts much pain. And after the monsoon's abated and the flooding relented, my ghosts boarded boats to trade the rice they had finally been able to grow. Except that the boats overturned, my ghosts lost their rice, and never found their way home."

"So you offer umbrellas to protect them from the rain?"

"Yes, but there is another reason too."

"What is that?"

"An umbrella is very handy. If you are on land it can protect you from the rain. But if you are at sea and your boat capsizes, you can turn it upside down and use it as a lifeboat too." A compassionate chuckle followed the man's comment.

"So an umbrella will always keep you safe?"

"Yes, an umbrella will always keep you safe."

Byrd smiled to herself and glanced out the door. Meimei stood next to a man with a stash of colorful umbrellas tucked under his arm. Half his size, she looked directly into the man's face, and he patted her silky head gently.

"You know what my papa says about boats?" Meimei continued.

"What's that?"

✓ "He says that boats honor the journeys of ancestors, a tale of valiant efforts and painful demise."

"Your papa is a wise man."

"He also told me once that my ancestors 'demised' on a boat." Meimei scanned the ground, placed her little hands on her scrawny hips, and peered up at the man again with a crooked neck. "I told him I didn't know what 'demised' means." Meimei glanced down again and scuffed her feet through the dirt. "Then Papa told me he would tell me when I'm older. I think I'm older now."

"Wait a few more years my girl, you're too young to understand." Kindness radiated from the man's rich voice.

Byrd stood with her eyes on the boat effigy and ears in the meditation garden. Slowly visual pieces of the puzzle slung through space to find their place on a timeline punctuated by boats.

She recalled that on her second evening visit to the Zhan's home to make effigies—amidst the elaborate ghost effigies spread upon the workshop table—a lone boat lay under the craft supplies, much like the one Byrd looked at now.

Further down the timeline, a cluster of boat images arose from her time in the Mekong. The first was a bevy of sampan's lingering outside the Lin's home as a neighborhood of family and friends, many of whom were Chinese, arrived at the house for the older sister's bittersweet homecoming.

Then there were the produce boats at the Floating Fruit Market, symbolic of the economic booms and busts of regional aquatic trade flowing in and out of the canals.

Finally, the timeline ended with an image of Byrd herself staring out on a destructive sea at the white hulls of two boats that crashed in the turbulent water.

Lost in thought, Byrd barely noticed the soft footsteps coming toward her from the garden. Though suddenly, Meimei stood before her, her hands hiding in her pockets and gaze fixed toward the ground. Meimei shuffled up the step then looked at Byrd. In that moment, the little girl's lost and forlorn expression finally revealed the subtle though potent detail Byrd had overlooked all along.

For the first time, Byrd looked at Meimei and understood the burden she bore—the hidden wounds of painful cultural and familial demise on a boat whose torrid rocking Meimei felt but did not have words for yet. Byrd's gaze widened when the real ghosts crept out of Meimei's eyes and into her own.

Byrd's head spun, she couldn't bear to look at Meimei anymore, fearful that the truth of what she saw might become apparent to the little girl—the invisible scars of a savage history that plagued Meimei's family, people, and culture still. Byrd diverted her gaze from the girl back to the boat. She shuddered at the effigy laying on its side, welcoming the ancestral ghosts back to a hard land from a desolate and drowning sea.

Byrd steadied herself in the doorway and gasped for fresh air. Meimei walked inside barely taking notice of the boat on the alter though it's presence still weighted her steps. Though still, Byrd wrestled to understand the historical connectivity between the Zhan family, other overseas Chinese, and boats.

Byrd recounted the history she had learned along the way and honed in on the time that still seemed murky. Qi Xiaofeng revealed the history of the overseas Chinese in Vietnam, but was fairly elusive about the past thirty years; Mr. Zhan's family perished in 1979 though Byrd never learned how or why; Mr. Lin's family also left Ho Chi Minh City in 1975. Even Vu's family left Ho Chi Minh City in 1975. Byrd rocked from her heels to her toes. *Nearly every overseas Chinese person I have met left Ho Chi Minh City in the late 1970s and has a bizarre aversion to boats. What happened to the overseas Chinese on a boat between 1975 and 1979?*

Byrd swiveled on her heels and walked in rigid steps toward the main door. She looked out into the courtyard and spotted Mr. Zhan chatting with an older man. Mr. Zhan caught Byrd's urgent gaze so he excused himself and met her in the center of the swarm of people.

"Mr. Zhan, I get it. Boats! Something happened to the overseas Chinese between 1975 and 1979 on boats, though that is as far as I can get. Please, fill me in." Mr. Zhan nodded with his hands behind his back and escorted Byrd to an empty bench.

"You've come this far, you deserve to know the details, but I'm warning you, it's a pretty grim story." After she nodded accepting that she still wanted him to continue, Mr. Zhan steadied himself on a weak bench slat and began.

"You already know the harsh reality the overseas Chinese faced as a result of the North gaining control of the South, right? Well, many overseas Chinese—and other immigrants, as well as southern Vietnamese for that matter—attempted to leave Vietnam. In 1978 a steady stream of people left these shores hoping to either re-migrate back to China or create a new home in more accepting neighboring countries like Thailand, Malaysia, and Singapore. In fact, the circumstances were so dire that departures by sea mounted for eleven years, and by the end, 600,000-700,000 people vacated the country."

"Now this wouldn't have been such a brutally fatal scenario alone, but the problem was that with little resources, these people were forced to leave in unimaginably small boats without any navigation equipment to brave the turbulent waters of the South China Sea." Byrd recalled the rough seascape off the coast of Ha Tien and nodded at Mr. Zhan's inference.

"Yet the harsh waters were only one plight the voyagers faced. You see, no one, including the Vietnamese government was very happy about the departures. Law enforcement and pirates alike harassed these boats at sea—they were under constant attack and their passengers were beaten, pillaged, murdered, raped—the worst. In the end, 100,000 people perished at sea." Byrd's eyes widened in disbelief as Mr. Zhan continued with the grim facts.

"What's more, when some of these passengers did make it to distant shores, a few countries refused them entry. In essence, these 'boat people,' as they've come to be called, left Vietnam for an uncertain future either way—they might make it to another shore, yet still, their future was uncertain if they did."

"Mr. Zhan, I had no idea…" Byrd didn't know what else to say, she felt an immense sense of guilt wrap around her heart for prodding him for details in the first place. "If I had known how personal these ghosts were for you, I never would have…"

Mr. Zhan interrupted. "Byrd, it's okay. You would have run into them no matter which Chinese family you happened to meet in Ho Chi Minh City. We have all been affected. Regarding our family—or at least our parents and siblings, aunts, uncles, and cousins—we Zhan's attempted to flee in 1979 and my family set sail in a boat from the Delta.

But only a few miles off shore, the boat capsized in an unruly police chase. This was actually a major incident—over 1,000 people died. The only survivors of 'Tra Vinh,' as that savage event has come to be called, were my brother and his oldest son."

Mr. Zhan steadied himself on the bench, Byrd leaned forward and swallowed. "I'm sorry, Byrd, I tried to warn you that this was a brutal affair."

Byrd rested her head in her hands and focused on a tiny white pebble between her sandals. When she recovered her sensibilities, she looked at Mr. Zhan. She wasn't sure what felt worse—the fact that she had been so selfish with her own desire to find the ghosts that she'd overlooked how intrusive her questioning might have been to the Zhan's; or the feelings that arose when she thought of what the Zhan's had dealt with themselves.

Mr. Zhan continued softly when he saw her façade weaken, "Byrd, I'm sure you see that these are not just familial ghosts—they belong to our culture at that specific time and place in history. So I don't take your questioning personally.

"In fact, many of Mr. Lin's ancestors perished as well. I doubt Mr. Lin told you, but his older sister was one of the lucky few to escape on a different boat with her first husband. Regretfully, I know she feels a great deal of shame for choosing the right boat, per say, while the rest of her family who fled did not. She hasn't returned to Vietnam since, it's simply been too painful for her. It's painful for all of us, but we survivors have each other."

"What about Mr. Lin? Did he not try to escape with his family, I mean, why is he still living in the Delta?" Byrd tried to focus on the facts to keep her emotions from heightening.

"I was never quite sure why Mr. Lin elected to remain behind. I can only guess that after he fled Ho Chi Minh City for the Delta initially, he was determined not to be displaced again." Mr. Zhan added, "What I do know is that many of his neighbors on that little island you visited made the same decision to stay. Many are Chinese and they clung together tightly during those tough times." Byrd recalled the Chinese lanterns in the bar—details started to make sense.

Byrd deliberated whether to probe further, but she remembered the gravity of her assignment and persevered—there were still a few loose strings she couldn't tie together.

"Mr. Zhan, this may seem like an odd question and I'm not even sure why it's popped into my head, but why, in the midst of all of this turmoil, did you suggest I visit the Floating Fruit Market?"

Mr. Zhan thought for a moment then snorted slightly and gave Byrd a half-grin. "I guess I wanted you to see the good aspects of the boats too—their emblematic symbol of mercantile trade representing opportunity for our people—both Vietnamese and Chinese alike."

Byrd nodded letting his answer settle inside. After a moment, she continued with a final question. "One more question Mr. Zhan. It's about Ha Tien. I mean, I realize you probably suggested I go there to find the cemetery, which Mr. Lin graciously directed me toward. And while it *was* helpful see it—to understand the overseas Chinese community's integral place in Vietnamese history..." Byrd's sentence trailed off. "Well, that's not what my question is about."

Byrd stuttered, "Let me try this again. What truly struck me most about Ha Tien was a woman I met there rather coincidentally. Vu's family had re-migrated three times—from China, to Ho Chi Minh City, to the Delta, and then finally to the U.S. in 1975."

"At the time I didn't think too much about the coincidence of that date, though I did notice that both you and Qi Xiaofeng alluded to 1975 in your history accounts. Well, now it's obvious, or at least very plausible, that her family were boat people too. Considering her reaction to the boats anyway..."

"Why do you say that?" Mr. Zhan asked. Perhaps there had been an unexpected twist in her time in Ha Tien that even Mr. Zhan had not presumed.

"Well, while we were eating, there were some boats below the restaurant resting on the beach. At one point Vu got up from the table and walked to the balcony railing. She watched the boats for a few minutes, then basically, up and left."

Byrd continued before Mr. Zhan could comment. "But what I can't piece together about Vu now is how her family eventually ended up in the U.S.? I thought you said the 'boat people' fled to other regions in Southeast Asia?"

Mr. Lin turned to face Byrd more directly on the bench. "I might be able to help you with that detail. In the 1980s many of these boat people were detained in refugee camps—from Thailand to Malaysia, to Hong Kong, etc. Many of these refugees eventually applied for asylum in countries that would grant it, namely the U.S., Australia, and Europe. That might be how this young lady made it to your soil."

"But she didn't mention anything about living in any other country before the U.S. after her family left Ha Tien. What would you make of that?"

"How old would you presume her to be, Byrd?"

"She alluded to the fact that she was a student doing research here, so I would guess somewhere between 22-24 years old?"

"Well, that would make her four years old at the oldest when her family moved to the U.S., so it's plausible that her family lived elsewhere beforehand. Perhaps in one of these refugee camps, though she was too young to remember."

"Often parents don't reveal scars of the past to their children because they fear it will hurt them, Byrd. You're not a parent, so you don't know that yet, but it's possible that you just met that young woman's ghost."

As Byrd accompanied Mr. Zhan home he asked, "What's next for you Byrd?"

"Well, the Meeting Place of Asia to greet the ghosts who won't respond to pity—*wherever* that is and *whatever* that means…'"

Byrd turned to Mr. Zhan, "I don't suppose you can offer any insight?"

Mr. Zhan smiled, slid his hands behind his back, and shook his head. Byrd knew by now that Mr. Zhan wouldn't be able to give any more insight than he already had, so she added, "I think I'll hop on an overland Chinatown bus tomorrow—keep following the lanterns. They've served me well thus far." Byrd smiled and Mr. Zhan laughed.

"Who has you on this assignment anyway?"

"My boss's name is D. Beak."

"She must be 'something,' it seems she's really thought this assignment through!"
"Why do you say that?"

"Well, I don't know. It's just that...I think I might have a sense of where she's steering you—from what I know about ghosts anyway."

He stalled, "I guess what I mean is she's likely an 'experienced' lady to have you on this task."

"I'll take your word for it Mr. Zhan, though at times I've considered her to be somewhat batty myself!" Byrd winked though this assignment truly made her wonder—this one was the most bizarre yet.

"In that case Byrd, you might consider a pit-stop with my brother's oldest son—Tang, the one I mentioned who survived the boat massacre. He lives in a city called Georgetown on the island of Penang, which is off the west coast of Malaysia. It's in the general direction you'll be traveling. If you can get there in one month's time, you could join him for the final Hungry Ghost ceremony. Georgetown has a robust and thriving Chinese population, so it should be quite a spectacle. He'd be a great resource for you."

"That would be fantastic, Mr. Zhan!" Byrd was grateful to have another trusted contact.

"Great, I will arrange the details with him. He knows quite a bit about the ghosts, I'm sure he'll be able give you some insight."

By the time Byrd and Mr. Zhan reached his celebratory nicknacks shop, it seemed there was little left to say. Except for thanks.

"Mr. Zhan, I really don't even know how to begin to express my gratit…" Mr. Zhan interjected.

"Please Byrd, you don't have to thank me."

"Well, then let me apologi…"

"Please Byrd, you don't have to apologize."

"But," she started again. She wanted to thank him for his time, resourcefulness, and guidance. She wanted to apologize for her constant probing—now that she knew how challenging it must have been to talk about these ghosts. Yet Mr. Zhan wouldn't permit it.

"Byrd, just do me two things."

"Anything, Mr. Zhan, what's that?"

"First is actually for you. Keep your head focused down and your chin up. Okay?"

"I think I can do that, thank you." Though in her mind, Byrd rectified that his suggestion was more easily said than done on this assignment. "What else?"

"Number two is actually for Lin Xiuzhan." He turned to face Byrd and smiled, "Please find her a nice Chinese-American husband!" Mr. Zhan chuckled and swept his arms around Byrd in a bear hug.

Byrd smiled though her heart strained, thinking of Lin Xiuzhan and her lovers in the park.

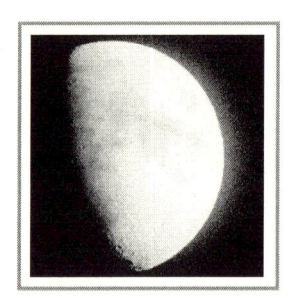

The journey up the coast was a wet and rocky ride. A typhoon licked the coast voraciously, chasing the bus up the seaboard with deluge rains, stymieing the trip for two consecutive weeks of nonstop gale force winds. The storm left the roads in miserable condition, not to mention the seats were cramped, and Byrd's ears rang from perpetual honking horns as the bus sped along the muddy overland route.

Byrd hadn't slept through the night since departing her sparse though comfortable oasis at the mini-guest house Ho Chi Minh City. She winced at each curve in the road and cursed the potholes pock-marking the unpaved route. Each time the reckless bus driver slammed through even the slightest watery dip, Byrd knocked her head on the luggage rack above.

She caught glimpses of dismal detail out the window —vast expanses of soggy landscape punctured grim city sights. At one point, the driver and his weary travelers plunged through the flooded streets of a small village stopping short of an accident in the middle of the road.

Two young men collided on mopeds. One bike was totaled and its rider had two gruesome scrapes on his leg. The other man appeared unscathed, though lashed out vehemently at the other in a heated skirmish on the dreary roadside. When neither had more energy to throw punches, they marched in opposite directions leaving their bikes on the side of the rode, their wheels still spinning.

Meanwhile a woman in a purple jumpsuit yelled at a girl in a pink suit under the awning of a dilapidated cafe building. An unattended little boy of approximately three toddled toward the bikes and cut a deep gash on his arm from a piece of loose metal. Byrd watched the red blood drip profusely from his elbow plunging into a brown puddle.

The boy's mother, the woman in the purple suit, scurried over and hit him on the forehead. He ran off crying into the ditch while she hurriedly scooped up as many spare bike parts as her arms could bear.

◐

While food and bathroom breaks at small roadside cafes broke up the overland journey, the pit-stops were no more restful than the ride. At one particular stop, Byrd hopped off the bus for a hot tea.

Content to have a moment's reprieve from her bus seat, she pulled up a wobbly chair at a dirty communal table where a meek Japanese female traveler sat. Byrd sipped at her tea when a boy and his blind mother approached their table.

The duo, tethered together by a frayed rope, hobbled over to stand on either side of the Japanese woman. Though it was hard to discern who was leading whom, it was the boy who haggled with the dainty woman to give him money for a drink.

When the women declined, the boy shoved his hand under her chin resolutely. He stomped his foot lifting a small cloud of dust, and demanded money again. When the woman shook her head no for the second time, the boy jerked his hand forward just centimeters from her nose. The woman backed her head away slightly, though looked down at her lap, refusing passively to give in. Finally the little boy slammed his hand on the table. The Japanese woman began to weep quietly and summoned a waiter for sugar to add to her coffee as a distraction.

Angered by the scene, Byrd barked at the mother and son to leave the woman alone. Bothered by their aggressive attack, yet saddened that they had to beg in the first place, Byrd walked out of the restaurant disheartened.

The walk to the bus was even worse. A little girl approached Byrd selling outdated postcard packs. Byrd knew these postcards well. Naively or gullibly—she wasn't sure which it was—she had purchased some from a ten year old boy her first week in Ho Chi Minh City. Yet when she returned to her room to write home to family and friends, she opened the postcard pack to discover one single image of Ho Chi Minh. The nine other 'fillers' were images of women in front of cars, Mickey Mouse, and the Eiffel Tower.

Since then, Byrd too had become adept at saying no to aggressive salesmen and the like. So when the postcard girl sauntered up to Byrd with a mischievous smile, Byrd responded immediately.

"No thank you, I don't need postcards today. Though you do look lovely in your dress." She hoped the girl would leave her alone with a compliment.

Apparently, the little girl found Byrd's comment unacceptable because she stepped on Byrd's toe with a forceful stomp and deliberate grind. "Pretty is pretty. It means nothing! It doesn't sell postcards!" The girl strut away to find another target.

Instantly Byrd became complacent. She's right. She grabbed the aches rising in her stomach with her free hand as hot tea scolded the other and she stumbled back onto the bus.

There, Byrd overheard a Parisian tourist jabber loudly to his friend about choosing one's preferred bus death. He gave three options: by asphyxiation of road dust, suffocation, or (with a sarcastic laugh) drowning if the bus rolled into a flooded ditch. Though his humor hit Byrd the wrong way, she wasn't in the mood for sour jokes and she scoffed under her breath.

One weary scene after another—day after day—Byrd felt trapped in a storm brewing in her body which raged for release. Desperate to persevere and follow the lanterns though exhausted, she decided to take a break from the road.

She disembarked impulsively at a small seaside town whose streets were flooded in four-inches of freezing water. As she walked up the main artery with water lapping at her ankles, a sniffly nose and no Kleenex, she scanned the street-scape buildings for signs of life.

Through the deluge she spotted a single building with a lit spotlight and tramped toward it. She shivered in the doorway, haggling with the hotel owner who tried to charge her double for the room because he surmised that her soaked feet might ruin his rug. It was a losing battle, there was no other place to stay in town that still had electricity, so she dropped soggy dong on the counter. She chugged up four flights of stairs to a dank and musty room and dropped onto a rickety bed. Byrd crashed with the storm outside.

When she woke, Byrd lay on the bed facing the ceiling—dehydrated with parched lips and a tongue as salty and dry as the Sahara in winter. She stared out the window at dirty and drab buildings of uneven heights and girths. Their weathered rooftop terraces were adorned with unkempt plants that rustled skittishly in the wind. Brooms swept water in and out of the street stalls below, each tender trying to keep her flooded space tidy; though litter, food scraps, and car parts floated down the flooded street.

Cold rain splattered on Byrd's pillowcase, so she moved away from the leaky window and curled up on the other side of the bed. Entranced by the tick-tock of an unsteady clock, wisps of hair fell on her forehead, blown by the chilling breeze of a fan whizzing precariously above.

Laying still for the first time since leaving Ho Chi Minh City, critters of all sorts jittered in her belly—cockroaches creeping with fear, bees swarming in anger, moths flying blindly, lightning bugs flickering on and off, and a rare butterfly flapping hopefully that tomorrow might be brighter.

Discouragement slipped sloppily in her head, attempting to grab hold of her fragile state of mind in the dark. Byrd reached for a notebook her sister gave her before she left home. She scribbled her thoughts out to dry across the barren page in simple verse:

*I'm tired. Haven't eaten a good meal in a while.*

Byrd stopped and let the ink pool in a black puddle on the page. She lifted her pen for a moment then continued in messy penmanship, supporting her head with her free hand.

*I found the ghosts in Ho Chi Minh City and have now traveled halfway up the coast in pursuit of them, but continue to slam into hardship: the suffering of others, of families, of culture—even nature's rips, rains, and tides. I am starting to feel lost myself.*

*Sturdy tangible photographs help me make sense of the world without absorbing the challenges and strife I encounter along the way. Without my lens, I am vulnerable to everything I see.*

*This assignment has me spinning like a toy top on the loose—bouncing off the table, landing with a thunk on the floor, bopping itself upright, and spiraling quickly toward the door.*

Byrd stopped writing and drew in a deep breath. She capped the pen and flipped back in her journal to an entry she wrote on a day when the nature of D. Beak's assignment made more sense.

*As ethnicities collide in a globalizing world and new melting pots emerge—brimming with migrants, refugees, and wandering souls alike—some cultures will inevitably slide to make room for new identities. So the question might be... How do we ride the inevitable wings of change amongst other nations, people, and within ourselves so as not to get in each other's way and fray humanity's heart?*

**Then Byrd found a side-note in the margin.** *Where is the world going with all of this suffering we impose on each other? Is it survival of the fittest or simply inhumane human nature? More importantly, does it serve a purpose?*

She shifted her posture to lie flat on her stomach, and placed the journal under her upper body propped up on her elbows like a cobra. She flipped to another entry she wrote the previous night by the dim light of the bumpy bus ride.

*Extract the pineapple juice from its plant to make the shake.*

Byrd couldn't actually recall writing the sentence—so she read it again. She must have been semiconscious when she scribbled it down. But as the storm pulled trees up by the roots outside, the single hopeful fragment cloistered between two larger brooding entries made sense. Byrd flipped forward to a blank page in the journal and sketched ten choppy lines:

*"The Amber Chip: A Lesson In Preservation"*
*The amber chip housed ancient insects.*
*Trudy and Franz dug it up in the forest dirt.*
*Lacandonian Indians danced on it for hundreds of years.*
*Now safe in the San Cristóbal Historical Center.*
*It's preserved in a decrepit old building,*
*Against the swarming mass of nomads who wish to see it.*
*Living organisms, culture, cities locked inside.*
*Which will be preserved? Which will deteriorate?*
*When the alchemist finds the chip,*
*Melts it, melds it, molds it—freeing the ghosts inside.*

Byrd set the journal down, suddenly realizing why D. Beak had sent her out without her lens. To truly find a new view, Byrd would have to *feel* what she saw without hiding behind the camera lens anymore. She would have to unearth whatever lurked inside the amber chip for this assignment. Yet still, the suffering she saw hurt. All she wanted was for it to stop.

After a full night's sleep, Byrd woke calm, soft, and tender inside—like a kitten. Not weak, but fragile and sensitive. She took two showers, one steaming hot to

*wushu moon magic*

seduce any residual despair out fro[m]
another not cool, but cooler to rel[ax and]
calm her senses.

More energized and hopeful to se[e]
through the rain, Byrd asked the innkee[per] what he
might suggest she visit.

"That easy," he said without skipping a line in his book.

"Go visit crazy monk-artist. He live in his own private pagoda."

"How do I find his pagoda?" The boy pointed toward a posting on the wall, which appeared the monk had created himself. The advertisement read, 'Take home memories from my Wushu Moon Pagoda.' The monk's proud stance and wide smile in the corner photograph beckoned to Byrd, so she started the wet slog up the pathway in the raw rain.

The pagoda was perched on a misty hill with a sign hung from a bamboo pole above the door—*Wushu Moon Pagoda*.

Byrd pulled her numb hand out of her poncho and rapped on the paneled wooden door. Feet scurried inside and a petite spectacled man peeked at her through a peephole before creaking the heavy door ajar. When he saw how wet she was, he ushered her in immediately, and Byrd smiled at him graciously. *gratefully,*

武术月亮魔术

...onk wore a thick brown robe with splatters of paint on the sleeves, and a large brown sack over his head. Black pointy shoes protruded from his long robe, though Byrd caught sight of stark white running socks bunched at his ankles when he walked.

Byrd took a quick glance around the pagoda—it had been hollowed out into a painter's studio. The lighting drooping from a cob-webbed chandelier above was dim, though there was one bright spotlight shining on an easel in a vacant corner. The rest of the pagoda was littered with paintings: stacked messily on the long scratched surface of the wooden dining table and cluttering nearly every square foot of the dusty wood floor. Other framed works rested against the plywood walls—seven canvases deep in some places!

"You want to see my brush paintings, right?" The monk half-asked half-suggested as he shuffled toward the table in the center of the room.

"Yes, the innkeeper tells me you have quite a collection." Byrd followed his small steps.

"Yes, a good collection. Perhaps you buy one of dragon, most expensive, and make me rich!" His body shook slightly with laughter though no sound came out. The monk then turned to Byrd, "You, Nomad of the Wind, what paintings you like to see?" Byrd laughed, acknowledging the perceptive accuracy of his statement from what she felt about her quirky assignment thus far.

"Well, I don't know, what do you have?"

"Come, I show you." He escorted her around to the other side of the table and whipped through a stack of ghoulish and grotesque images in sweeping black calligraphy mounted on colorful silk scrolls. Byrd was taken aback, the images were astoundingly haunting, like Münch's 'Scream,' far from the serene images she'd expected to find.

"Well, I was thinking something a little more 'upbeat,'" she stuttered. The monk swiveled to face her briefly, then gazed up at the ceiling, and picked up a paint palette laying on the table.

"Come here, talk while I paint." He shuffled over to the easel and motioned for Byrd to sit on the stool behind it. He dumped black ink into the palette's centerpiece and etched quick strokes on the page.

"Why you not like these paintings?"

Stunned by his blunt question, Byrd batted her eyes. "Frankly Monk," she knew it sounded ridiculous to call him that, but didn't know how else to address him, "I've been under a sky that's let loose on me for days now, and I'm tired of it." She was surprised by her own sharp reply.

"You don't like rain?" He retrieved a fine-haired brush from the depths of his gown, dipped it in a Dixie cup, and glanced at Byrd.

"Actually, I love the rain." She looked around the room and continued talking, "In fact, I remember its first burst upon my arrival in Vietnam. It was an absolutely breathtaking moment, really, watching the rain splash the city silly." She recalled the details of her first monsoon pleasantly, "Listening to it dance on the tin roof—tap, razzle, pop—as it poured in sheets from the awning I stood under." Byrd stopped abruptly when she recalled disappointedly that she didn't have her camera handy to snap a shot.

The monk looked up from his work briefly, acknowledging there was more she wished to say, and nodded encouragingly with a smile. "Go on."

"I guess I'm just a bit discouraged at the moment by an assignment I'm working on."

"So you want upbeat?" The monk set his palette and brush down, then stood peacefully with his arms at his side.

"Yes, I guess a glimmer of light."

"I might have something for you." He swung the easel around for Byrd to view his latest work. Byrd rose from the stool to her feet, awed. It was a simple though beautiful rendition of a little lantern hanging over a river's edge.

"But how did you know? How did you know that I've been following lanterns?" Byrd was astonished by his subject choice.

"You don't want to buy dragon painting—yet. You don't like ghost paintings either. The only other option is a lantern," the monk offered casually. Byrd bowed gratefully though she was utterly perplexed by the monk's sixth sense—for lack of a better expression.

The monk bowed back then suggested "Okay, 20 dollar." He smiled sheepishly, "Everyone have to make a living you know."

Byrd did know. She dug a crinkled American dollar bill from her wallet and handed it to him with an incredulous though slightly amused look. The monk thanked her for the money then buried it in the fold of his dark robe. Abruptly, he scurried toward a closet.

His voice echoed from its hollow depths, "Now I give bonus gift!" He popped out of the closet with a long brush and jet-black ink stone. "Use these to shadow box like Wushu warrior when you have to fight something you cannot yet see." He smiled and nodded in delight handing the objects to Byrd

Again perplexed, Byrd stumbled for a response. "That's extremely thoughtful, but I'm not much of a painter....I wouldn't know where to begin."

The monk interrupted, "No, not painter, Wushu Warrior."

Byrd frowned, "I'm sorry, I don't understand."

"You tell me you want to see a glimmer of light on a rainy day. First you begin with what you think you see—maybe rainy day. Then you shadow box like Wushu warrior to fight what you cannot see—maybe sunshine hiding behind clouds. Finally, you finish with what you truly do see—maybe you come back and tell me what that is someday." He smiled and stood proud of his analogy.

Byrd looked at the little man skeptically, baffled by his kind gesture. She tucked the painting, ink-stone, and brush into her poncho pouch. With that, the monk gave her a firm pat on the back and shepherded her toward the door. It slammed before she could ask him anything else. She stood in the drizzling rain speechless for a moment, uncertain what to make of her encounter. *What a crazy old monk!*

Byrd turned on her heels and raced down the hill in long slippery strides. Something about the absurdity of the encounter offered a ray of light, a playful touch of madness, that inspired her to continue. *Perhaps I do need to fight what I can't yet see.*

When Byrd resumed her perch on the bus seated against another cold windowsill, she stuck the ink-stone in her pocket and wove the brush through her hair to make a loose bun. As the bus lunged west through the countryside toward the other coast, Byrd clutched the canvass in her lap. She hoped it would inspire her to venture forward on a trail of lanterns heading in a new direction.

Over the next few days, the rain abated encouragingly the further the bus traveled from the typhoon-ridden coast. On the first clear dawn two days into the journey, Byrd spied a flaming yellow ball lift a jet-black night into a deep azure-blue sky. The early morning light slipped up a funny-shaped mountain like a loose fitting skirt and Byrd found the conical mountainous landscape of Laos.

By midmorning the mountains drizzled on the horizon like upside down pineapple cake frosting, dripping out of the light blue sky and into the lush green foliage below. A rippling tree canopy rolled below the mountains in perfect symmetry with the peaks above. The beautiful landscape ruptured Byrd's senses and tore down the desolate views she had seen days before.

Each day Byrd found something invigorating to see out the window. When the bus motored through a small city early one morning, she witnessed hundreds of teenage boys with shaved heads, bare arms, and sandaled feet lining the streets. They were garbed in orange robes and each carried a gold offering pot slung over his shoulder. Byrd learned from her guidebook that the little monks-to-be of Vientiane collected alms every morning at 5 am.

When the bus lurched into Bangkok, Thailand, suffocated in smog and gritty splendor, Byrd hopped off the bus scouring for a lantern. Sure enough, as she followed the river a few hundred yards from the station and crossed the street, she found a narrow grid block speckled by the familiar lanterns of Chinatown! She stopped at a dumpling stand, ordered six to go, and hopped back on the bus—assured that she was on the right track.

As the bus maneuvered through the city, Byrd observed that Bangkok's architecture was like any other modern international hub, though a few exceptions poked out of the drab view like little buried treasures. Byrd delighted in the diverse array of A-frame wats with pointy gold roofs and Buddha statues rising to the sky out of lotus leaf thrones.

One elaborately tiled roof caught Byrd's eye in particular. A meticulous pattern of red, yellow, and green shingles on six interconnected buildings matched the cover image of a magazine she'd picked up. *Yes, it was the Royal Palace!*

Architectural splendors like the palace, wats, and Buddha statues whet Byrd's visual appetite. Yet when the bus finally careened back out of the city sprawl down the coast of Thailand, she realized that it was truly Southeast Asia's natural scenery which inspired her most.

There she looked out on an ocean speckled with islands resembling little men with green domed hats and ruddy sand-colored faces. As sunlight filtered through the clouds above, the fickle sea changed color like a chameleon—from light green to aqua to deep blue. The steady lap of the ocean painted curious tidal patterns in the sand. Byrd ached for her camera to capture the arresting scenes.

There was only one image on her journey down the coast which struck her as fairly nondescript—the gates of the Thailand-Malaysia border patrol office. Though too, when it loomed in the distance, Byrd was grateful because this meant she could give her eyes a much needed rest while passengers hopped off for a bathroom break.

As the bus zoomed toward the station, Byrd calibrated the vast expanse of land in front of her—it was much larger than she'd realized. Finally a half hour after she first spotted the border gates on the horizon, they arrived close enough to its façade for her to make out its individual cement blocks. As the bus jumped the speed bump at the first gate and passengers disembarked, Byrd let her drowsy eyelids flutter shut.

Twenty minutes later when the bus's engine rumbled toward the exit gate, Byrd rubbed her eyes. She glanced up at a white banner with a wild cat emblem—perhaps a tiger or a puma. As the bus rolled beneath it, Byrd squinted at the banner's red lettering. It read 'Welcome to the Meeting Place of Asia...where all cultures cross!' Byrd couldn't believe it! She'd begun to wonder if D. Beak had used poetic license, and the Meeting Place of Asia wasn't actually a real place at all.

By mid-afternoon the bus traveled at a steady clip along a well-tended road that cut a path through a verdant green oasis. Byrd leaned into the aisle for a panoramic view through the broad front window of the bus. The landscape looked like the Great Plains of her own country: 20% sweeping grassland and 80% open blue sky. As the sun set, the expansive sky dazzled in deep red, orange, and purple hues like a Hawaiian sunset. Mile after mile, she was mesmerized by its kaleidoscope, one beautiful cloud-filled image shifting into the next—taking on new shape and form as the bus thundered along.

It surprised Byrd how sparsely populated this Meeting Place of Asia appeared to be. The bus had cruised through the rolling terrain for hours and still she hadn't seen anyone, not even a water buffalo or bird. And yet, as the bus wove through the landscape at the same rhythmic pace, one hour slipped into the next without a soul in sight.

Yet on the final eve of her bus journey, Byrd spotted an odd shape that broke the contiguous scene in the distance. As they drew closer, she made out the details of a flaming cauldron sitting dead-center in the middle of a rice paddy. Its fire shot brilliant orange streaks toward the sky. *But this lantern was the real deal!* Puzzled, Byrd had no idea what purpose it served or who lived nearby to stoke it.

As the bus zoomed along, the cauldron dropped into the distant horizon out the back window before the mystery was solved.

A few hours later, the bus rolled up to a small dock. Byrd watched a double-decker ferry lurch toward the mainland and lunge lazily into port. Within minutes she was aboard, speeding toward Georgetown on the island of Penang to meet Mr. Zhan's nephew Tang.

Tang's appearance caught Byrd by surprise when he rounded the street corner and greeted her at the entrance to the Malaysia Hotel an hour early. He was a small puffy man garbed in a tailored suit with brand name sunglasses wrapped around his squinty glee-filled eyes.

"Byrd, that looks heavy!" Tang held out his hand, "Here, let me help you with that." He was shorter than her, but appeared sturdy and capable.

Byrd smiled, "Normally I'd decline your offer, but I'm exhausted! Look at these toes!" She pointed down at her weary feet flipping out of loose flops, grimy with traveler's sludge from one month on the road.

Byrd's comment and Tang's subsequent laugh broke the ice and the conversation continued casually.

"Welcome to Malaysia!" Tang offered with a smile exuding both joy and success as he propped the heavy hotel door open, leading her into an air-conditioned lobby.

"Yes, thanks! I see now that it's the Meeting Place of Asia too." Byrd winked realizing that Mr. Zhan knew a visit to Tang's home would lead her to the next clue all along. Tang nodded then chuckled through heavy wheezing bellows.

Byrd turned to Tang, "Am I late or are you early?"

"I'm early, finished with a client and thought I'd sit at the bar and enjoy a drink before you arrived. So please, don't let me rush you. Take your time and get settled in your room." Tang dropped Byrd's bag with a bellman and steered her toward the reception counter with a pudgy index finger.

"Thanks Tang, I would like to shower. I'll be back down in twenty minutes."

"Great, you'll know where to find me." Tang straightened his suit, bowed slightly and strolled toward the bar top. Byrd checked in, showered, and was back down in the lobby by the time Tang finished his first Cosmopolitan.

"That was fast, Byrd!"

"I've adapted to speedy showers these days, the water pressure hasn't been so great on this leg of the trip."

"I can't imagine that it has been. Then again, you hardly need showers with all the rain you've passed through. I've been watching the storm since my uncle advised me of your departure from Ho Chi Minh City. It's been one of the worst monsoon season's in quite some time."

Byrd slipped into a stool to join Tang at eye-level. "Well, I have to say I'm happy to hear that. Honestly, the rain was starting to bring me down. I'm glad to hear that's not an every-year occurrence...if it were, I'm not sure I'd come back!" she joked though was fairly serious.

"Besides the rain, how was your journey?" Tang inquired.

"A little bumpy at first, but I made it." Byrd thought to spare the details for a 'rainier' day.

When the bartender noticed that Byrd had joined Tang, he approached, drying a glass in his hand. He beckoned to Byrd and she ordered a glass of house white.

"I hope you don't mind but my uncle informed me that you've been on a photography assignment to capture the Hungry Ghosts?!"

"Yes, 'capture' is a good way to put it," Byrd chuckled as Tang continued.

"So, what have you found thus far?"

Byrd hesitated, sizing Tang up. *Perhaps he is the sort of guy with whom I can be blunt, like Mr. Zhan.*

"Well Tang, these ghosts—these 'boat people,'" she hesitated again.

"Go ahead, Byrd. I am completely comfortable talking about this. Please say what is on your mind."

"Okay, good." Byrd was relieved to hear that Tang was receptive to chatting about the grim history of his community. "Well, it strikes me that you all—the overseas Chinese, I mean—worked so hard to settle and create opportunity in Vietnam, yet endured so much suffering. It's been hard to see. I can't imagine what it was like to live through."

Tang nodded objectively, as if it had not been his family and people who had struggled. Byrd continued, "The painful loss of family history and culture—due to war and a changing external world. And now it's even worse, I imagine, what with globalization that can make mincemeat out of cultures with the flick of a switch... It seems there was so much struggle, seemingly so unjust...."

Byrd knew she was rambling but continued, "I suppose because I came to know your family quite well, that I felt their pain far more personally than I had anticipated. Far more personally than any other assignment I've ever been on, frankly."

Tang responded simply, "I can imagine."

When he was silent, Byrd continued, "Yet what perplexes me, Tang—and what I'm still grappling with—is that the overseas Chinese are extraordinarily resilient. They go here, there, everywhere to set up shop—literally. Yet at the same time, they are still inextricably linked through strong cultural traditions to mainland China.

So it's odd. It's obvious that the overseas communities are still built on the cornerstone of Chinese beliefs: self-reliance, righteous Confucian values like thrift and discipline, family cohesion and education. And yet, they are somewhat exiled from their roots because they have chosen to settle elsewhere in lands where those dogmas may or may not exist. It must be a fairly isolating environment, especially in cases like what happened in Vietnam with 'Tra Vinh.' They worked so hard for a better opportunity, yet got slapped in the face."

Tang sat back as if *he'd* just been slapped in the face. Suddenly Byrd was ashamed of her comments, perhaps they were a bit harsh.

After a long breath Tang suggested, "Wow Byrd, you paint a pretty grim picture."

"Well, isn't it?" She asked in a softer voice, less confident of her summation.

Byrd backtracked, "Look Tang, I came here on an assignment, but admittedly this experience has struck a chord with me. I've found it personally distressing to see. Perhaps it's because…" Byrd decided to sidestep the fact that she didn't have her camera to hide behind on this assignment—thus she reeled even more in the painful images with no way to capture them. "It's just been more personally challenging than I had imagined, that's all."

"Perhaps that's the point, Byrd. After all good photographs aren't found in history books, they're often found in coffee table books. I'm sure you know why that is."

Byrd looked at him quizzically, so he continued with his theory. "Good photographs are personable, that's why they are stacked on living room tables rather than sidelined on bookshelves."

Tang sat back and took a delicate sip of his drink, "But back to the point, let me offer you the silver lining for the overseas Chinese here in Malaysia, so that our history doesn't appear so dismal to you. It doesn't end in Vietnam, Byrd. Our history doesn't end with 'Tra Vinh.'"

Tang's eyes darted from left to right in their sockets as he reflected on an appropriate entry point for his sentiments. "Byrd, let me tell you about the history of the Chinese in Malaysia."

*Here we go again...*

"I'm going to give you a quick summation because we have an exciting night ahead of us, but here is the gist so that you can start to connect the dots." Tang unfolded his hands from the bar top and placed them in his lap while Byrd muttered in her head. *Good Tang, short and sweet. Please keep this short and sweet.*

However, Tang persevered slowly and meticulously. "Historically, many Chinese migrated to Malaysia overland across the border in the 18th century, similar to their initial migration to Vietnam. Also similar in some ways to Vietnam, the overseas Chinese came up against third party rule that resisted their presence to a certain degree—the French reign in Vietnam and British rule here in Malaysia."

Tang took a sip of his second Cosmo, crossed his legs, and put his glasses in his breast coat pocket. He continued, "On some occasions, it is true that the overseas Chinese got caught between traditional roots grounded in homeland ideology and a new land whose reign found this ideology inappropriate. So it is fair to say that the overseas Chinese got stuck between a rock and a hard place, as you alluded to."

Byrd laughed cursorily, finding it amusing how frequently her new friends drew upon American euphemisms. Though when Tang's serious expression didn't change, Byrd did her best to match his demeanor.

Quickly, she added, "But it sounds like what you're saying backs up my theory earlier, so I don't see the silver lining yet."

"Ah, but!" Tang held up his finger then clasped his drink. "Malaysia is an interesting case because the overseas Chinese represent nearly 30% of the country's population. So most of the society on this small island is largely of Chinese origin to begin with. On Penang, many overseas Chinese are still fluent in the native tongue, and many Chinese cultural and clan associations are still fully intact."

Byrd listened intently searching for the silver lining while Tang continued. "Yet it's the multiculturalism of this land coupled with the burgeoning number of Chinese who live here that has helped the overseas Chinese community to blossom. We live here, work here, have advantageous opportunities here—in most sense, we are rooted here. However, we have also still been able to maintain our traditional customs because they are largely accepted here."

"In fact, many of my friends still retain strong financial and cultural ties to mainland China, but the threads are manageable because we are reasonably accepted here. It has taken some time, but we are a more established population than Cho Lon now, so there are many differences."

"I think I'm starting to understand. So would you say that depending on the local 'freedom' the host country lends, the Chinese are plagued by varying degrees of tension between their roots and their new land?"

"Precisely, Byrd! Thus acceptance is the key—to anyone's survival anywhere actually."

By now, Byrd was on track and in sync with Tang's history lesson. "That's intriguing theoretically, Tang, but perhaps if I understood where you were coming from, I might be able to follow better. If you don't mind me asking, what about you—what is your story here?"

"Well, I gather you know all about my family's ill-fated migration from Vietnam to Malaysia."

Byrd nodded.

"Yes, my family are 'boat people' and what we endured is tragic. Yes, I am the only living survivor. Yes, when my father and I arrived in Malaysia, he worked repairing shoes for less money than he had before he set sail for this country. And yes, he died a very sad man. And yes, that makes me sad. Do not get me wrong, I carry the ghosts of this history—perhaps now more than ever because he has died and there is no one else I can share them with who will ever truly understand. But over time my thinking changed about the whole matter."

"How?" Byrd and Tang had barely moved since their dialogue began, but now Byrd realized her foot had fallen asleep, so she shook it under the table while Tang continued.

"Well, let me put it like this... When I was a boy, my father took me to the Hungry Ghost Festival. I don't recall if I ever went before we emigrated from Vietnam to Malaysia, but I distinctly recall him taking me to the performance here one year.

"Actually it's the very same performance I will take you to tonight. Anyway, it was there that my father told me about his ghosts. Even then, I still had no idea whom or what he was truly referring to, but I figured it out with time."

Byrd sat up straight, "What did you figure out with time, Tang?"

Tang shook his head. "Byrd, I'm sure you've heard this before, but you'll have to figure it out on your own too. That said, the myth of Mu Lian will help."

"Okay Tang, then what is this myth of Mu Lian? It must be very potent to have helped you so much. You seem so happy, joyous, and successful here now—after all you have been through."

"Come, Byrd. Let's explore the final Hungry Ghost Festival! You'll meet Mu Lian there."

Tang led Byrd down a crowded street where hundreds of people strolled in the direction of a large square marked off by red ribbon. En route, they moseyed past neighborhood streets decorated with elaborate table offerings, each honoring paper ghost effigies propped-up on the tabletops. Elaborate jigsaw puzzles of fake money sat in uniform rows on each street corner, their surfaces scattered with dainty red, yellow, and orange flowers.

Finally Tang and Byrd arrived at the backside of an outdoor venue, where families lay sprawled out on a wide sidewalk waiting for the opera performance to begin.

As a wiry music ensemble began, Tang led Byrd around to the front of the stage where a smoke machine billowed around bright yellow silk scrolls hanging from bamboo partitions. Spotlights sparkled and colorful rays of blue light emanated from the stage floor into the steel-frame ceiling above.

Those audience members who elected formal seating sat densely jammed in plastic chairs anxiously awaiting the performance. However, the first row remained empty. Tang explained, "Those seats are reserved for the Hungry Ghosts. Come, let's sit back here," he suggested, selecting two seats in the last row.

"Byrd this is a long performance, probably three hours. Sometimes a little laborious, but hang in there, it's worth it." He winked.

The opera began when a young actor of about twenty years dressed in a fire-truck red suit stepped onstage. Red eye shadow fanned up his white forehead in spirals and two straggly pigtails grazed messily on his shoulders. In typical Chinese opera fashion, his costume made it difficult to discern if he was meant to play the role of a man or a woman. Though from what Byrd understood about Chinese opera, the androgyny of the characters was intentional because the stories were more about particular themes than the characters themselves.

As eerie music twisted over itself in the sultry night air, the actor approached a fiery dungeon or jail cell at center stage where a single figure stood. The female prisoner's hair was streaked with long silver and white strands, which sparkled in the stage light as she writhed up and down the prison gates in trancelike moans. The emotion on the man's pained face when he caught sight of this woman was riveting —suggesting that it was someone he knew well behind the bars.

The man and woman had a brief conversation before he promptly darted off the stage through a plume of swirling smoke. As the lights morphed from red to blue, then purple to black, the woman's jail cell spun around as if perched on an oversized lazy Susan— conveying a short passage of time.

Then the man returned to the women's cell bearing food and clothing, and hastily handed them to her through the bars. Though when she touched them, they went up in flames—a dramatic effect the stagehands pulled off well. The man ran off the stage again, and the jail cell spun around a second time. Though this time, the dungeon backdrop was replaced by a simple throne and a seated Buddha.

When the man returned to the stage, the placid Buddha smiled at him. It seemed from the man's expression that he pleaded with the Buddha for something, yet the Buddha shook his head in disagreement. At this point the story-line confused Byrd, so she leaned over to Tang for elucidation.

"Tang, what's happening?"

Tang caught her up to speed. "That's Mu Lian, a monk disciple of Buddha, who is trying to rescue that woman, Pu Ma, from hell for her evil doings. As you saw, Mu Lian brought her provisions, but everything Pu Ma touched went up in flames."

Tang paused for a moment, recounting the details of the story-line then continued. "So now what you see is Mu Lian asking the Buddha for help to release her. Though the Buddha just told Mu Lian that he himself couldn't save Pu Ma, there is still one thing Mu Lian can do. We are now at the point in the story where the Buddha will reveal to Mu Lian what that is." Tang rested his hands in his lap satisfactorily, and straightened himself in his chair to redirect his attention to the stage.

The young man returned with a cluster of garbed men dressed like the Buddha in robes. One carried a basket of provisions while another held a traditional Chinese instrument in his hand. The scene unfolded as the monk disciples prepared an elaborate feast complete with candlelight and dazzling food platters.

"What's happening now?" Byrd whispered to Tang.

Tang waited for a brief pause in the accompanying music then turned to Byrd. "Mu Lian has gathered some friendly disciples to help him perform seven rituals that will help save Pu Ma."

As the performance continued, the disciples munched on the scrumptious food while working together to create seven elaborate effigies one-by-one.

After each effigy was created, Mu Lian held the duty of lighting them on fire—bringing the inanimate objects to life. The scene unfolded slowly though meticulously. As Mu Lian lit each effigy, a booming gong clanged behind stage. Byrd realized that the scene was somewhat similar to the ritual she had observed at the pagoda in Vietnam.

Finally, the disciples presented the seventh effigy to Mu Lian—a large black feline with green eyes. Cautiously, Mu Lian lit the cat's tail on fire with an overdramatic stroke of his wand, and the gong clanged twice, its echo reverberating dramatically through the night.

Immediately the stage lights flickered—red and pink lighting flashed madly across the stage and into the first few rows of the audience. The disciples wobbled back and forth in their chairs as if an earthquake shook the ground. Suddenly the platform upon which they stood shifted left and Pu Ma's cell glided into view on rickety wheels.

The music stopped and the disciples' movements froze. The gates of Pu Ma's cell opened, their rusty hinges screeching. Huddled in the corner of her cell, Pu Ma watched in awe then rose to her feet dramatically.

She took two sweeping glances to ensure that no one was watching, then crept closer to the doorway of her cell. She stood under its frame and a red light glowed beneath her, illuminating a frail profile underneath her boxy garb.

Then she spotted Mu Lian across the stage, as if he'd arrived out of nowhere. Pu Ma's eyes welled with tears as she looked at him—full of sorrow and regret. He too, was frozen, his hallowed expressionless face illuminated by the light of the glowing feline.

Pu Ma bowed toward him deeply, her nose nearly touching the ground. Then with unfettered gusto, she darted from her cell and tore down the stage steps through the audience aisle, and sprinted down the main street of Georgetown. Her ghost was free!

The crowd stood on their seats, chanting, cheering, and whistling! As the curtains closed, the audience filed out rapidly from their seats.

"Where are they going?" Byrd asked as she turned to watch the crowd amble toward the street.

"To burn money for their ghosts before nightfall." Byrd watched in wonder as the audience turned into actors themselves. They lit heaps of plastic bags packed full of paper money on the sidewalks, which tumbled like molten lava into the street.

One man tossed a ghost effigy onto the burning pile outside his home, then threw another plastic bundle of money on the pile. Suffocated by the plastic, his ghost wheezed as all of his money, not to mention his appendages, went in flames.

Within ten minutes, the entire street was ablaze—flames rose everywhere—as the neighborhood audience freed their ghosts on the streets. White buildings glowed pink in the red light—at once Georgetown became a city of destruction and delight.

Tang leaned toward Byrd, "Did you like that, Byrd?"

"Well, yes, it was quite a performance, but I'm still not sure I follow the story-line."

With flames rising behind his head, Tang filled in the details for Byrd. "You see, as I mentioned Mu Lian was a monk disciple. As a young boy, he showed great promise to achieve stature as a monk. However, Pu Ma, a woman we regard as someone close to Mu Lian—though it is never precisely clear who she is—does everything she can to sabotage his greatest desires.

"As Mu Lian grows older and is just one step away from becoming a monk, he learns that Pu Ma has been imprisoned. Yet at this point, he still does not know that it is actually her that is standing between him and his desire to become a monk. So when he learns that Pu Ma has been incarcerated, he goes to visit her in prison immediately. And this is where the opera story-line begins.

"When Mu Lian arrives at the prison gates, Pu Ma finally reveals to him that she is the one sabotaging his efforts—thus causing him so much pain. At first, he is outraged, then he is hurt and full of sorrow. Under great duress, he goes to visit the Buddha to resolve how to handle his suffering. On this visit, Mu Lian learns something very important about Pu Ma."

Tang took a breath, "Are you following me, Byrd?"

"I think so."

"Okay, good. You see, what Mu Lian comes to realize after his conversation with the Buddha is that Pu Ma is sabotaging his efforts for her own self-interest. It's not that she truly wants to hurt him, it's simply that she felt that if Mu Lian became a monk, she would lose him from her own life. So Pu Ma does everything she can to prevent his monk-hood.

"Once Mu Lian understood this, that the pain Pu Ma caused him was truly because of her own fear of loss, he began to have great compassion for her. Not that it made any of the acts she did justifiable, but Mu Lian understood her motives better."

"I see," Byrd offered hesitantly, though she imagined that if she were Mu Lian, it would take a lot more than one conversation with a Buddha to help her have compassion for someone who did something so malicious.

Tang noticed Byrd's reservation but continued with his explanation. "Look Byrd, Mu Lian had to make a choice. He could leave Pu Ma to suffer for eternity at the gates of hell; or he could free her, so that he could free his own heart from the wounds she had inflicted. In the end, he decided that keeping her chained up did him no good either. He made the choice to go with compassion over revenge."

Byrd thought about Tang's words while she watched the embers burn on the street. Still she wondered why Pu Ma would want to hurt Mu Lian in this manner and how he could possibly forgive her.

It seemed Tang read Byrd's mind because he continued his commentary, "Byrd, KNOW this— *Again*, Mu Lian realized that Pu Ma feared losing him so deeply, that she actually foiled his attempts to pursue his calling as a monk disciple. *Yet* when he realized that it was her LOVE—though misguided as it was that led to her actions—Mu Lian's heart filled with compassion."

It was his exuberant compassion that finally allowed Mu Lian to forgive Pu Ma—sick and grotesque as she behaved. This is what ultimately helped him to set her free."

Tang sat back seemingly satisfied that he had reached the end of his explanation. Byrd leaned forward preparing to reply, but nothing came out.

"Okay Byrd, let me put it like this. We have all suffered from something, right? We have all been hurt by someone, right?"

Byrd nodded so Tang could continue.

"Well, suffering—which is really just grief-stricken pain—is what happens when someone clings to pity—either for themselves or for another. The Buddha helped Mu Lian to see that responding to suffering with pity would lead nowhere. Pity traps negative feelings in the heart. But compassion—compassion is what releases the pain, anger, guilt, regret, and fear."

Tang stared at Byrd directly and offered one final thought, "What you must see, Byrd...rather, the moral of the story is that Pu Ma caused Mu Lian a great deal of pain. As a result he suffered. YET, Mu Lian did not want to hold this suffering in his heart. He wanted to let it go so he could move on with his own life and become a monk. He realized if he didn't, all the negativity would swallow his heart. So he chose to let it go. BUT it was only through his own suffering that eventually Mu Lian found compassion. If he hadn't been hurt by Pu Ma, he may not have learned this lesson—one that we all must face at some point."

"If you want my personal take," Tang smiled at Byrd and she smiled back because she knew he would gladly give it, "It's all about the powerful duality of love. Some of us know how to love without hurting others. Some of us don't. As a result, we suffer from time to time. However, we also love—all the time. It's just that sometimes it comes out in twisted ways.

"Unfortunately, in the case of some people with intense pity, pain, vengeance, or jealously trapped in their heart—malicious, even unlawful acts can be committed. Think of war, hate crimes, discrimination, even family feuds, bullying on the playground...it's all the same. You get the point.

"But even these people have a chance, if they can find a way to love compassionately again. Does that make sense?"

Byrd looked at Tang skeptically so he continued.

"LOVE drives our every action. It's our FEAR of not receiving IT—or of being hurt by another, one-upped by another, or being replaced by another—that gets in our way. That's just what makes us all the same. We are all human in that sense."

He chuckled then added, "We love. We lose. We lose. We love. Chinese, American, African, Hindu, Catholic, Jewish, or Christian. We're all the same." Tang sat back in his chair—finally, he truly was satisfied.

Byrd leaned forward resting her head in her hands. She turned to face Tang sideways and smiled—at first just a slight grin and then a wide rapturous toothy smile. She was comforted by this man's wisdom hiding under such a cool facade.

Byrd kept her response simple. "Tang, I get it. Intellectually at least. I've got nothing more to offer than that you are right at this point."

In that moment, Byrd saw her assignment in a different light. The Hungry Ghosts weren't overseas Chinese 'boat people,' they were simply people-people. Any human who suffered any loss—of love, opportunity, money, family—just plain old loss and was grieving still.

Luckily, Byrd saw hope—there were those who had come out the other side of a long dark tunnel. People like Tang, bursting with reverential compassion to help others along the way.

Byrd and Tang sat in silence for some time as an acrobatic troupe walked onstage for the final scene. As the troupe set up an assortment of apparatus onstage, Byrd turned to Tang, "So is Pu Ma the King Ghost's wife then? I mean, he seems to get a lot of attention for the Hungry Ghost Festival as the 'Big Cheese,' but you never hear anything about his wife."

"Well, everyone has their own interpretation, but I'd say you're onto something Byrd. After all, don't you Americans have a saying that behind every great man is a great woman? Or something to that effect?"

Byrd laughed, "Something like that. And Pu Ma was in the limelight tonight!" Byrd winked though she wasn't sure if she'd translated the joke well enough into Chinese for Tang to understand, but it didn't matter. They both laughed, watching a gentle breeze sift the heaping ash piles sideways across the street.

Finally a burst of firecrackers ripped through the night sky over the squat row of houses, and the character of Pu Ma raced up the street. She lifted her gaping gown to her knees, and leapt up the stage to take a final bow. The acrobats lifted her into the air and launched her into a triple somersault, and then she landed on her own feet. The actor was greeted with more cheers and whistles from a standing ovation.

Tang turned toward Byrd and winked, "Pu Ma might be a ghost or she might just represent the dark side of us all, our own ghosts. But I'll say this, she gets to me each time I see this performance." Tang winked then turned to face the street, now littered by heaps of grey ash. He scanned the scene looking for something, then spotted it. He bowed peacefully toward the lone King Ghost effigy still burning amongst the rubble.

Byrd watched Tang's gesture with intrigue. The festival seemed to have an authentic place in the overseas Chinese community's reality, and yet it was all a staged effort—even to the degree that Pu Ma freely ran down the street! It was so real and yet so surreal—she had never seen anything like it.

Yet still, there was one aspect to the evening that was completely authentic—the raw evocative emotion the Hungry Ghosts evoked from both the opera performers and the audience alike.

And finally with the help of Tang, D. Beak's second clue made sense. *Ghosts surely didn't respond to pity—that would never set them free. Though compassion, compassion might...*

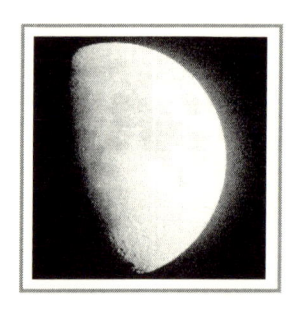

Byrd was still lost in thought when an Indian man with sparkling eyes startled her by slipping into an adjacent empty seat. Byrd glanced at Tang, who leaned forward and poked his head around Byrd's shoulder. His eyes widened in delight, and he stuck out his hand toward the man. "Bala, great to see you my friend! I'm glad you could make it!"

"Yes, though it appears that I missed all the fun. Can you believe the wedding is still going on? I had to dodge two aunts, an uncle, one cousin, and a feral dog to get here to see you. The exuberant Indian man wiped glistening sweat off his forehead. "Is this your uncle's friend?"

"Yes, I'm sorry, Byrd meet Bala. Bala has come home to Georgetown for his cousin's wedding. We were classmates long ago, before he became too successful for Malaysia and moved down to the big city." Tang winked at Bala.

"Nice to meet you, Byrd."

"Likewise," she took his outstretched hand and smiled, captivated by the most intriguing eyes she had ever seen. The man's retinas were pure black, not chocolate or dark brown, but black like ink. Their darkness created a mesmerizing effect, so that the white corneas sparkled even more than she had seen in any other eyes of a lighter shade. She dropped her gaze and was relieved when Tang spoke.

"Byrd, let us walk you back to the hotel." My home is in that direction and Bala is also heading that way."

"Thank you." The threesome strolled through the street still smoldering from the offerings.

"Where will you go from here, Byrd?" Tang asked, sidestepping a heap of ash.

"I'm continuing down the coast to wrap up my assignment in the City by the Sea. There's a third clue that I must resolve." But before she had a chance to think about it, Tang interjected.

"Which one, there are quite a few Cities by the Sea."

Uncertain, Byrd offered vaguely, "The one at the end of a string of red lanterns?"

Bala chimed in, "Ah, Singapore, you mean? That's where I live! I can drive you if you like—save you a bus ride. Plus it'll be quicker by car." Bala and Tang grinned at each other sharing an understood smile. Byrd thought about the previous bus rides—uncomfortable seats and hideous music—and found the answer easily.

"I'd be grateful Bala, thank you." Byrd and Bala smiled at each other, as the threesome rounded the street corner where bellowing drums and snakelike music emanated from an exquisite temple.

The tacky red and white striped façade didn't do much for Byrd, however the artistry on the temple's rooftop—featuring mythic freeform figures caught in a frozen diorama—piqued her interest. Her eyes scanned the entryway, picking up horizontal blue, white, and pink stripes that wrapped around its ornate columns.

"Sri Mahamarianman, here's my stop." Bala cued and pointed over his shoulder toward the open entryway of the elaborate façade.

Standing directly in front of the arched door, Byrd found mystical Hindu Gods and Goddesses lurking in small alcoves just inside the entryway. She traced their slender forms up to the pink lotus leaf in relief on the ceiling. A long chain of metal links dropped from its pistil in the center suspending a chandelier.

The flower was surrounded by four out-of-place angels that looked down onto a tiled floor, seemingly oblivious to the miscellaneous strands of wired lighting dripping from their toes. Yet even this intriguing view paled in comparison to the vivacious jubilee Byrd found inside the temple.

She zoomed in ogle-eyed at a bride with white-teeth and a brilliant smile, her youthful eyes sparkling in celebratory joy. She appeared to be about twenty-one years old, nervous and weary of all the attention, yet pulsing with the loving energy of a bride-to-be. Byrd imagined the honey suckle woven through her hair smelled as beautiful as it looked, dancing on a crown on her head.

A slightly older woman, possibly the bride's sister, stood weighted to one side bolstering a baby on her left hip. A little girl of approximately ten years cradled the baby's cheek in her pudgy hand. When she cooed woefully, the little girl swept baby's face up toward her auntie in white, and her eyes fixated on the bride's beautiful face.

Byrd's eyes zoomed out to take in the scene overall. The wedding party stood under a canopy of frilly flowers on a floor cushioned with Malay palm fronds. The bride and groom, important relatives, and a cameraman invited an endless receiving line through the canopy.

Byrd zoomed in a final time, marveling at the elaborate details of a gaggle of women passing through the receiving line. Royal purple, saffron yellow, and blush red saris, held together by strands of gold, draped off their dark bodices. The fabric wove through arms, across foreheads, looped midriffs, and swept delicately across henna-covered hands. The splendor of these regal women sparkled from delicate gold jewels on every wrist, ankle, ear, nose, and neckline.

Entranced by the crowded temple scene, it took Bala two attempts to draw Byrd's attention back to the street.

"Byrd?" Byrd stood still, mesmerized by the scene inside the temple, so Bala gently clasped her elbows. "Byrd? I'll pick you up tomorrow morning, let's say 9 am?"

Finally she focused on Bala's lips amongst the loud music blaring from the temple. "Yes Bala, 9 am."

Bala smiled. Finally she met his sparkly gaze, refracting shards of light like crystal, and was stunned speechless when she found that his eyes were even more intriguing to her now than moments before.

With an innocent passing glimpse into his family and his culture through the doorway, the source of spark in his eyes made more sense. It seemed world's away from the suffering she found weeks before.

Immediately, she looked down at her feet, embarrassed, though she smiled when his hand grazed her shoulder. There was something about those eyes...extraordinarily seductive though curiously, they also sent shivers down her spine and invited goose bumps on her skin.

Byrd stood in front of the Malaysia Hotel the next morning and looked at her watch wondering what kept Bala, when she heard popular western tunes booming from a perpendicular street.

An engine revved cantankerously and Bala sped around the corner in a low-riding black car with tinted windows. He honked the horn with two brief blasts, waved to Byrd through an open sunroof, and leaned over the passenger seat to open her door before the car rolled to a full stop.

Byrd looked in on Bala sporting a gaudy pair of yellow shades that elicited a smile on Byrd's face. She offered a morning salutation to her new friend—a quick hug—and slung her bag into the back seat.

"Morning Byrd, how'd you sleep?" Bala inquired as Byrd strapped herself into a plush though firm black leather seat and Bala swerved back into the stream of commuter traffic.

"Well, I slept through the night, but I guess I have a lot on my mind. I woke a bit weary."

"Well, then I have something to pep you up. I noticed you enjoyed the music outside the temple last night, so I burned this for you." He handed her a CD.

"Bala that's so kind. Shall we listen to it?"

"Sure, pop it in." Byrd inserted the CD into the deck and an Indy-rock song started slowly. Hollow percussion and slithery synth sounds were paired together like a mismatched misfit; though jingling bells and wobbly sitar chords complemented the rhythmic chanting of high-pitched female voices perfectly. The entrancingly seductive rhythms brought a fresh smile to Byrd's face as they sped through the city island toward the ferry.

"I could get into this," Byrd smiled at Bala sideways. By the time they arrived at the ferry dock to make the voyage back to mainland Malaysia, they'd listened to the CD in its entirety twice.

Bala rolled the car onto the vessel over a rickety ramp, and followed the parking attendant's flag toward a row of small automobiles squeezed between two packed tourist buses. "I'm so grateful that I'm not on that bus, thanks again for the ride Bala."

"Don't mention it Byrd, I'm happy to have the company." He slowed the car to a stop and turned off the ignition. The car lights dimmed but the music continued.

"How was your cousin's wedding anyway?"

"Oh, the usual. Very festive, lots of dancing, even more drinking. It was nice to see my Granny." Bala smiled and placed his hands in his lap.

"Do you come home often to visit?"

"Not that much, I suppose. I'm quite busy with work in Singapore these days."

"Is that why you moved there?"

"Yes, I started a technology business there with a friend about five years ago. Malaysia may be known as the Meeting Place of Asia, but Singapore is the gateway to the international business world these days."

"Why is Malaysia known as the Meeting Place of Asia anyway?"

"Oh probably because it's quite multicultural and has been a major trade post between countries for some time. Everyone passing through Southeast Asia inevitably trickles through Malaysia."

"But you think that Singapore is the international hub these days?"

"Yes, respectively speaking it's a young country, only a couple hundred years old, but it's arguably the most developed Southeast Asian city, so it made sense to start our business there."

In the intimate setting, the words between Bala and Byrd became more academic. Byrd reminded herself that she was on an assignment after all, though she was curious about this fellow.

"Do you like living in Singapore, Bala?"

"Sure, there is always something to do and I have some great friends. I do feel bad leaving my Granny behind in Georgetown though."

"You're close to her?"

"Yes. My parents died when I was young and she's cared for me since I was four."

"I'm sorry to hear that." The music buffered the lapse in conversation for a moment before Bala continued.

"And you Byrd, with all the questions," Bala turned toward her placing his hand on the headrest of her seat, "you have come far from home. What assignment brought you to Southeast Asia?" His eyes glistened in the dark, the effect nearly more potent than in the daylight.

Byrd glanced away quickly, then jumped when a loud thud pounded on the trunk of the car. Both Bala and

Byrd spun around in their seats to catch the parking attendant's impatient gaze. Apparently cars had begun to vacate the ferry but they hadn't noticed. Bala turned the car on swiftly and wheeled it back with a squeak, waving to the attendant for the inconvenience.

He spun the car around, slid back down the ramp onto mainland soil, and shifted into second gear speeding south on Route 1.

"Bala, how long will it take us to get to Singapore?"

"It's about an eight hour drive, seven on a good day."

"Wow, that long!?"

"Yes, is there somewhere you have to be?"

"Well, as I mentioned, I have to find the last red lantern for my assignment, though I'm not certain where it is. I just want to make sure I have sufficient time to find it."

Bala thought for a moment. "I'm pretty sure I know where it is, I'd be happy to show you."

"Really? That would be fantastic! Have you been there before, to Chinatown, I mean?"

Bala glanced at Byrd quizzically. "Sure Byrd, I've been to Chinatown many times, but that's not where the last lantern is." Byrd turned to Bala with an expression of sheer fright.

"What do you mean, the last of the lanterns isn't in Chinatown? I've been following Chinese lanterns all the way to get here on this assignment." A dreadful thought crossed her mind, "Have I been on the wrong path all along?"

Bala saw the fear in Byrd's eyes and clutched her hand gently. "Not to worry, Byrd, the last lantern isn't in Chinatown, per say, but I'm fairly certain that the one you are referring to is the same one I am thinking of as well."

Byrd sighed in relief, though was still extremely concerned. "Well, can you take me to the one you know? I guess I'll know if it's the right one when I see it."

Bala smiled, "Yes, you should know if it's correct when you see it." He grinned and pushed his sunglasses into his thick black hair. He shifted gears and glanced at Byrd long enough for her to see his eyes sparkle again. They captured a hidden happiness or knowing that hooked her more with each glimpse, a contradiction to the bland view ahead.

The road stretched for miles through a clear-cut tunnel of trees—flat, paved, and nondescript. An occasional service station dotted the landscape, but that was it. As they traversed the mundane landscape and Bala zoomed down the desolate road racing other automobiles, Byrd's head wobbled in the cradle of her seat belt until she fell asleep.

Byrd awoke from a deep slumber to the sound of bleating horns and grating breaks in a new city. Bala noticed her slow movement and greeted her eagerly, "Good afternoon, you woke just in time!"

She smiled, her eyes still closed, "For what?"

"For a great view of the Petronas Towers, the tallest buildings in the world." He pointed out the window as her eyelids shimmied up in slight flutters.

Byrd shifted still semi-comatose in her seat to face the street, then leaned forward cranking her neck one-hundred-eighty degrees. She looked up at an enormous pair of shiny skyscrapers towering above the urban scene—the view altogether different from the one she dozed off to hours ago.

The space-shuttle-like statues rose up in a glassy façade flanked by geometric patterns and were linked midway at an enclosed walkway. The buildings terminated in fine needlepoint tips thousands of feet in the air.

"Wow!" Byrd lapsed back in her seat and looked at her watch.

"Yes, wow is right. They are about 1,500 feet tall. Unfortunately many of the floors are still vacant, they can't seem to rent out all the space."

"Wow!"

"Wow, what now?"

"I'm sorry, I'm still dazed. Where are we? How long have I been asleep?" then she added embarrassed, "I'm so sorry Bala, I should have warned you. I'm a horrible traveling companion when it comes to cars. Ever since I was little, something about the ride lulls me to ZZZ's."

"Not to worry, Byrd. You woke up at just the right time. We're in Kuala Lumpur, the capital of Malaysia, about halfway to Singapore." The traffic picked up and Bala steered the car along Jalan Ampang Avenue.

"Are we stopping here?" Byrd asked gawking at an increasingly tangled web of city streets pockmarked by treacherous gutters.

"Yes, I thought I'd take you to one of my favorite lunch spots."

"Do you travel through Kuala Lumpur often then? I mean, to have a favorite lunch spot?"

"Well, occasionally I come through on business, but not that often. Though whenever I get the chance, I go to a very special place my Granny introduced me to as a child."

"Well, how did she find it, being from Georgetown?"

"It's a long story, I'll tell you over lunch. We're nearly there."

An endless swarm of motorcycles snaked in and out of jolting cars and jerking buses as Bala lurched the car into the heart of the city toward what appeared on a signpost as 'The Golden Triangle.'

Suddenly Bala gunned the car left and headed up a one-way street into oncoming traffic. "Don't worry, pretty normal thing to do around here," he suggested, focusing intently on the intersection ahead. Bala made the hairy drive through the city an amazing feat a heroic act of sportsmanship—and finally slammed to a stop by a small side street.

"Here we are! Come on Sleepy Head," he smiled kiddingly, "let's get some, how you American's say, grub?" Byrd chuckled as she swung her car door open and it screeched against the top of a gritty sidewalk. Bala's command of English slang amused and amazed her. Byrd climbed out and met him in front of the car.

"Bala where did you learn your English? It's so... real."

"I watch a lot of American movies and soap operas," he smiled proudly.

"It's served you well. I feel like I'm talking to my friend, Peter, from home."

Bala squeezed Byrd's hand, pleased. He led her down a crumbling sidewalk at a steady pace, tugging her through a maze of business professionals and the occasional tourist toting oversize plastic shopping bags. Petaling Street burst with knockoff designer clothing: T-shirts, souvenirs, pirated videos, fake watches, and sunglasses.

"I'm so excited for some yummy Indian food, Bala. I can't remember the last time I had Indian."

"We're not eating Indian," he offered nonchalantly and continued through a market bizarre.

"Sorry? I assumed we'd eat Indian because I thought you mentioned your Granny introduced you to this place."

"She did," he offered casually, "but she's not Indian."

Confused Byrd asked, "I assumed she was?"

"No, she's Chinese."

Byrd stopped in place jerking Bala back slightly.

"But you don't look Chinese. I mean, I'm sorry, that shouldn't matter, but..." She picked up her pace to find its sync with Bala's steps again.

"Don't worry Byrd. I'll explain more at lunch, but she's not really my grandmother either, not by blood anyway."

Bala stopped in front of a small decrepit building, the outside appeared dingy—a true hole-in-the-wall next to the elegant restaurant next door. Bala swung the door open and cool air enveloped their hot bodies.

"It's no five-star restaurant as far as the ambiance is concerned, but the food is amazing. I promise!" He kissed his fingers like a French chef then winked.

When Byrd's eyes adjusted to the dim cavernous lighting, she found a myriad of red lanterns hanging along two long walls leading to a kitchen. *Back to the lanterns, at least that's a good sign!*

After a waitress seated them, Bala ordered promptly without peeking at a menu. When the waitress walked away from the table, Byrd pulled in her chair and leaned forward.

"Okay Bala, I'm lost, fill me in. Your grandmother is Chinese, though obviously not by blood. She lives in Penang but introduced you to this restaurant in Kuala Lumpur. Everyone has greeted you by name since we arrived. What's the scoop?" Byrd figured Bala could handle any slang she dished his way.

He smiled and leaned toward her across the table, "Okay, the whole truth and nothing but the truth." She smiled at his wit. "My mother is actually from KL. In fact, if you walk just a few blocks that direction," he pointed over his shoulder, "you will run into Little India where my mother grew up. Hence the 'Golden Triangle'…"

Byrd blinked, "Indian, Chinese, and Malaysian communities, you mean?"

"Exactly! Anyway back to Granny. The story starts when my mom was in her teens. She had a bit of a restless spirit, shall we say. She used to sneak out of the house in the middle of the night. On one particular night, as she used to tell the story, she had a strange hankering for dumplings. So she crossed over from Little India into Chinatown. Well, the only restaurant that was open at that ungodly hour was this one. She stood right there and gazed in."

Bala pointed down to the ground just below the window. "It was so late that most of the lights were off and there was only one woman left in the restaurant.

"As my mom recalls it, the woman was bent over her mop scrubbing the floor so fastidiously, that she hardly noticed my mother rapping on the window. Though finally, the woman turned around. Well, my mother gave the poor Chinese lady quite a fright. The woman jumped up startled, knocking over her mopping bucket, and slipping on the wet floor."

Byrd's eyes widened, Bala had to be making this up! He realized she didn't believe him, so he offered, "Verbatim Byrd, verbatim." Byrd realized that this probably wasn't precisely the word he meant but she got the gist.

"Anyway, when the Chinese woman finally stood up and stomped toward the door, my mother was still standing at the windowsill with her hands clasped around her mouth. My mom recalls that she thought this woman was going to hit her over the head with her mop!" Bala smiled and looked down at his hands.

"Well, the details always get foggy from there, but somehow my mom coaxed this woman down from her ranting and they sat on the stoop chatting all night. When the Chinese woman learned that all my mother really wanted to do was try a dumpling, she let her inside to pick at the leftovers. Long story short, she let my mom into the kitchen that night too, and actually taught her how to make them herself!"

Byrd smiled, "What a fantastic story, Bala! So I presume the Chinese woman is your Granny then?"

Bala's eyes glistened, "Yes, the Chinese woman was Granny. My mother and Granny became fast friends after that and my mother made many mad dashes out of the house when her family wasn't looking to taste Granny's scrumptious dumplings."

"It's too bad she's not here so I can try them for myself," Byrd added.

"Well, these are still pretty good. It was a family recipe. It was Granny's parents who actually owned this restaurant."

Bala raised his water glass to his lips giving Byrd an opportunity to pipe up. "But sorry, Bala, how did Granny end up living with your family in Penang?"

"Oh right. Well, my parents had a prearranged marriage, but they didn't have an arranged nanny. So when my mother moved in with my father, she insisted that Granny come too. He was hesitant at first, to have a Chinese nanny in an Indian household, but my mother was rather dictatorial when she needed to be. She wanted Granny and that was that. So Granny came to housekeep in Penang, then she took care of me when I was born."

"I'm really sorry I never had the chance to meet her Bala." Byrd sat back from the table.

"Me too, Byrd, you would have liked her. She's really the one who raised me, you know. After my parents passed away, Granny raised me the only way she knew how, which was somewhere between her own Chinese customs and those Indian customs she picked up from living with my parents for ten years before they passed away."

Byrd swallowed and sipped at her glass letting the cool rim linger on her lips. She wanted to ask Bala how they died but restrained herself.

"Anyway, I hope you like our meal, Byrd." Bala unraveled his wooden chopsticks from a paper napkin and changed the subject. "You should know that this restaurant is known as one of the best places around for authentic Guangdong cuisine! And you know what's great about Guangdong cuisine..."

"No, what's that?" Byrd asked as an array of colorful steaming plates arrived at the table in the hands of a friendly waitress.

"People from Guangdong believe that anything that walks, crawls, flies, or swims should be eaten. Most Chinese would agree, but those from Guangdong take it to the extreme. Take this platter, this is called 'Dragon and Tiger Fight.' It's actually braised snake and leopard." Byrd's mouth gaped open and she looked at him through wide incredulous eyes.

Bala continued, "And this one is braised phoenix liver and snake slices. It's stir-fried shredded snake meat in five colors. See one, two, three, four, five." He pointed to the variations of green, yellow, and red on the platter. Byrd stared at the dish uncertainly.

Bala caught her gaze, "You seemed adventurous, I thought you'd be eager to try some of these specialties?"

"I am Bala, I love trying new things, but some of these animals are endangered and that doesn't sit well with me. If there's only one hundred of something, I'm kind of of the mind that my stomach can pass on it." She scoffed jokingly though was entirely uneasy about the meal placed before her.

"Granny says that these animals aren't eaten all the time, but that they serve medicinal purposes, so we should take nourishment from them when they are placed in front of us."

Uneasy, Byrd picked up her chopsticks and snapped at a fleshy piece of snake meat. She smiled at Bala and offered, "Very unique!" She didn't want to insult him and it did taste okay, sort of like chicken. Deliberating uncertainly for a moment, Byrd rationalized that the snake was already dead, so she latched onto another piece with her chopsticks.

Bala and Byrd picked at the food until they were both moderately satiated and had more energy to chat, then Byrd spoke first.

"Bala, your story is so interesting. Would you say you know more about Indian or Chinese culture?"

He reflected for a moment, "Truthfully, Chinese. But that's an interesting question. I mean, I'm an Indian boy born on a Malaysian island and grew up with a Chinese granny. I think it's safe to say I'm what you Americans call a mutt."

Bala sat back, "When I think about it, perhaps that's why this restaurant appeals to me. The tastes and flavors transplant me home to a country which is not my own, but the closest thing I know to 'home.' If that makes any sense...perhaps that's why I moved to Singapore. The multiculturalism suits me well there and I am free to create my own home."

Byrd smiled at the face of an <u>Indian man with a Chinese head on his shoulders</u> who was creating his own roots in a new country to begin the cycle again.

"Bala, tell me what you know of the Chinese in Singapore."

"Tell you about the Chinese in Singapore, huh? Let's see."

"Singapore has the largest majority of Chinese inhabitants outside of China, even more than Malaysia. I think it's about three-quarters of the entire population these days.

"Though I think our president would be the first to attest that Singapore is not simply another China. On the contrary, he's extraordinarily proud of the multiculturalism that exists in Singapore. I remember a speech he delivered last month suggesting that Singapore should take a full day to celebrate all of its citizen's traditions, those of Chinese, Malay, and Indian alike. He wanted to make it a holiday, in fact."

Byrd was ravenous for more detail and scooped up what Bala knew as she grazed the final layer of sticky white rice in her bowl.

"Bala, do you think Singaporean's truly feel the same way?"

"About what?"

"Well, do you think they'd agree with the president? It seems like Singapore is the utopia we all seek in our minds, where multiculturalism rules the day and everyone gets along. I'm sure that sounds trite, but you know what I mean." Byrd picked up a grain of rice with her index finger and dropped it on her tongue.

"I'd say, yes, for the most part people would agree. Sometimes the government can be a bit rigid about its strategies to maintain and preserve its ethnic diversity, so no one gets marginalized, but on the whole I have to give the country credit because it seems to be working."

"What do you mean when you say that the government has rigid policies?"

"Well, in the past 30 years, when the country went from no organization to the tightly run nation that it is now, the government controlled nearly every aspect of society. For instance, when they built the housing units that 88% of Singaporean's live in, they went to great lengths to ensure that each housing community mimicked the precise percentage of the population overall. So in turn, in each housing unit, you will find 76% Chinese, 7% Indian and 14% Malaysian."

"Well, what happens if you have two more kids than you intended and you're Malay?"

Bala implied the obvious, "As I said some would argue these government strategies are too rigid."

"I'd say! I can't imagine what it would be like if my family had to move from one neighborhood to the next simply because my parents opted to have more children."

"I suppose we all get used to different standards."

"Yes, but the challenging thing about that claim is what happens when two cultures clash and there is no defiant government to 'strongly advise' everyone to get along." She threw quotations where needed and sat up assertively, thinking again about the 'boat people.'

"You know I've thought a lot about this issue on this assignment. Bala, you're smart. You get it. But don't you think the problems that arise when cultures collide isn't about erecting a temple here or a mosque there—it's about human interaction—human feelings?"

Byrd added a different twist to make her point clearer, "You, with all of your unique attributes, you are more joyful than anyone I have met. Do you ever feel lost in all of your diversity, or that you don't have a singular home? That there are parts of yourself or your heritage that even you don't understand? That even you don't know how to share?"

Bala looked like he was prepared to respond so Byrd sat quietly. Then he laughed shyly and offered, "Love affair with the moon, I suppose." He shrugged, laughed again, then grabbed her hand and pulled her toward the door.

The final leg of the trip was quiet and peaceful. Bala and Byrd didn't say much until they drew close to the Singaporean border.

"Byrd, when we get into the city, I'd like to invite you to try mooncakes. I think you'd enjoy them."

"I'd love to Bala, but I am a bit pressed for time to find the last lantern."

"You'll have plenty of time, I promise. You can't come to Singapore during Chinese Mooncake Festival and not at least try a mooncake. It's like coming to Singapore and missing the Sling. In addition you do have to eat dinner at some point, don't you? These are heavy little monsters. Eat one and it will tide you over for two meals. I promise. Mooncakes, then straight to the last lantern."

Byrd did enjoy Bala's company, so she asked, "Okay, tell me this, what is a mooncake anyway?"

"It's a round flat pastry made of a thin flour called snow-skin."

"Snow-skin?"

"Snow-skin. These pastries made of snow-skin are then filled with a paste made of salted egg yolk, rice flour, and lotus seed."

"Lotus seed? Is there really such a thing?"

"Yes Byrd, lotus seed, from lotus plants." Bala smiled then continued.

"The doughy concoctions are cooked and pressed, typically in a circular mold to give them a moonlike shape. They can be filled with red bean paste, nuts, jelly, yam, fruit, you name it. Nowadays they are also filled with vanilla flavored cream cheese, chocolate, the list goes on. And there are all kinds, really. Some are crispy on the outside, some are smooth, some round, some with ruffled edges." Bala's voice trailed off then he added, "but I promise, we won't try any with endangered animals inside."

"Good Bala!" Byrd stalled and thought for a moment. *He's so charming, how can I not?* "Okay, then I'll try it. But then straight to the lanterns, Bala." She jibed him but her clammy hand on his shoulder suggested she was serious.

Bala careened through a main intersection, then followed thick yellow traffic signs on the paved streets to an intersection steeped in opulence of European architecture. He turned right down a tree-lined street, then swiftly slid the car into a parking spot and wrestled with his seatbelt.

"Wait right here." He swung the door open, slammed it shut, and walked down a clean brick sidewalk in long swift strides. Though she hadn't noticed it before, Bala's head struck Byrd as disproportionately large for his lanky physique. It wasn't that he was entirely emaciated, though extraordinarily thin and gaunt in the face.

Bala stopped in front of a break between two stately columns then disappeared from view. When he hadn't returned in nearly twenty minutes, Byrd's curiosity got the best of her, so she hopped out to explore the street-scape herself. She walked toward the columns where Bala entered and stood in front of a massive food fair in an open-air market.

Above a sea of browsing consumers, a large red banner pulled taut between two buildings welcomed visitors to the Mooncake Festival in glittering gold Chinese characters. Ornate octagonal red lanterns—an obvious upgrade from the simple red balls she'd found on her overland route—hung from sturdy wrought-iron poles.

Long rectangular tables covered in red tablecloths stretched seven streets deep, covered by a plethora of intricately designed rectangular boxes. A vendor stood behind each table, making recommendations to people milling from one stand to the next about which tooth-picked treat to taste next.

Byrd spotted Bala's yellow shirt in the densely packed crowd walking toward a vendor. He pointed to a box, exchanged it for money from his wallet, then placed the change in a tip jar. He walked with his head down out of the market, lifted it to cross the street, and spotted Byrd. He dodged a rumbling van and two bicyclists to meet her on the sidewalk.

"Here, these are for you!" Bala handed Byrd the heavy ornate red box with gold encasing. As they walked back to the car, Byrd lifted the cover to find four intricately designed mooncakes individually wrapped in delicately thin red paper with a moon imprinted on the top.

"I went for the assorted pack so you can taste them all."

"Thanks Bala, that's kind. Why didn't you ask me to join you? That looked like fun."

"Because there is an even better spot to eat mooncakes!" Torn between the enchanting adventure Bala lured her on and the pending details of her assignment, Byrd looked at him skeptically.

When they arrived at the car, he opened her door and dashed around the front to his side. "I know, I know, Byrd. Just a few mooncakes and then I'll take you to the last lantern." He winked and ducked into the car before she could throw him another unconvinced stare.

Bala parked the car a few miles northwest of the city in an empty parking lot. He popped the trunk and withdrew a wool blanket, then flipped his sunglasses down from their perch in his tousled hair.

He glanced at Byrd, "Ready?"

"I guess so." Though she wasn't certain for what.

They crossed a bridge sturdy enough for a car though intended for foot traffic, and walked toward a welcome board implying that they had arrived at the 'Chinese Gardens.' Beyond the signpost, a red wooden archway opened into an expansive and well-manicured green swath of land, covered in recently planted trees and shrubbery. Traditional Chinese architectural motifs connected by groomed walkways decorated the park.

"Here, come this way Byrd. I think you'll enjoy what's up ahead." Bala led her along the pebbled walkway through an elaborate rock garden, interspersed with bonsai trees potted in ceramic urns. The view from above might appear like the rocks and bonsai were engaged in a giant game of chess.

"Wow Bala, this is fantastic!"

"I thought you'd like it here."

They meandered slowly along the path and through the garden to a miniature koi pond where an elder Chinese gentleman with wispy hair sat perched on a rock playing the *erhu*, a traditional Chinese string instrument. His long sweeps across two taunt strings mimicked somber weeps and his expression matched the sorrowful tune.

Byrd and Bala stopped to listen for a moment, then continued toward a miniature pagoda. They strolled through an arched doorway and descended upon another artificial koi pond.

They leaned over the pond's railing and peered down at freckled neon orange fish swimming lazily in and out of each other's paths. Byrd and Bala watched for some time before talking, as the fish darted into the far corners of the pool.

Stepping back from the railing and onto the pathway, Byrd finally turned to Bala, "What's next?"

"Eating mooncakes, of course!" Bala took Byrd's hand and led her though an open field of soft, nearly delicate manicured grass. Byrd took her shoes off and walked in bare feet.

"It's been so long since I've walked around without my shoes! My feet have grown so sensitive, it nearly tickles!"

Bala smiled and scooped Byrd up and swung her around to his back for a piggyback ride. She was surprised by his strength. For such a slight figure he was incredibly strong. He ambled for a few yards with her hunkered to his back, then stopped abruptly.

"Here, this is our spot." Bala released Byrd gently then spread a wool blanket on the ground. He took his shoes off and smoothed the surface of the blanket before lying down.

Byrd dusted off her feet then joined him, laying at a diagonal angle. Their bodies an arm's length apart, Bala and Byrd watched an arrow-shaped cloud move across the expansive sky. When it finally collided with an oblong cousin, Bala sat up and retrieved the box of mooncakes.

He dropped the box lightly on Byrd's stomach, "Which would you like to try first?"

Byrd sat up and investigated the box's contents. She lifted its top to read details on each cakes' ingredients. "Let's see, we have one with mango, cashew nuts, chestnuts, and lotus paste. Another with ginseng, bird's nest, and white lotus paste. The third is vanilla flavored cream cheese and macadamia nut. And finally," Byrd paused, "this one seems bland compared to the others. Durian?"

Bala smiled, "Oh the timeless durian mooncake! Simple, yet tantalizingly sinful. And made of a smelly fruit!"

"Oh right, durian fruit!" Byrd laughed recalling the first time she smelled durian at a fruit stand in Vietnam—the best description of its aroma being a foul trash bag floating in a putrid sewage alley.

"Let's go with the durian!" Bala jibed and pulled a plastic knife out of his pocket. He cut it into eighths and handed Byrd a hefty slice. She nibbled at its gooey interior.

"What do you think?"

"Not bad, heavy. Different." She chewed more thoroughly, "Bearable." Her nose flared in disgust. "That one is *not* for me. That is atrocious!" Bala laughed, then selected the ginseng, bird's nest, and white lotus cake.

"Let's try this one instead." Though after the second mooncake—which was also a bust—Bala suggested something different.

"Come Byrd, maybe mooncakes aren't for you. There is something else I want to show you." Eyeing the sun drop slowly though steadily toward the horizon, Byrd hesitated.

"Bala, I really should find that last lantern. I have to finish this assignment. Look, it's getting late, the sun is about to go down."

"That's right. The sun is about to go down. Timing is everything." Bala smiled, "Byrd, I promise I will get you to your last lantern." He pulled her to her feet.

"All right Bala, this time you win. But really, then straight to the last lantern."

Bala and Byrd walked along another pristine walkway into an open expanse where tacky cartoon-like figures dotted the lawn in staged animated scenes. Shaped with bent wire, they were wrapped in some sort of Teflon reflective cloth and dyed in a variety of ostentatious colors—neon pink, royal purple, sun yellow, and blazing orange.

"Bala, this is horrendous. What are these?"

"They're decorations set up around this time of year for yet another festival. But really what are they? Western world's influence on an unfettered land, that's my take," he joked.

When they reached the first scene, Byrd saw what Bala meant. The popular western fairy tale figure Snow White and her seven dwarves had come to Singapore. The fairy tale princess held a basket woven of brown Teflon, and stood frozen mid-droop to the ground to pluck a daisy. Surrounded by her furry friends—rabbits propped up on their haunches—the scene made for a good laugh. Meanwhile fish swung from the branches of a large tree above, and bats zoomed across zip lines—lending an even more surreal feel to the traditional legend.

Bala led Byrd along the path amusedly as she scoffed at the distasteful and egregious lawn ornaments. They ambled toward the next exhibit mimicking a lush garden with gaudy oversized flowers. Pink petals with purple stems grew forty feet from the grass toward the sky. Wire stars dangling from the flowers caught a slight breeze and glittered in the sunshine.

"Are these supposed to be flowers or palm trees?" Byrd asked Bala who chuckled at her snide sarcasm.

The path continued toward another scene, an animated veldt teeming with wildlife where typical zoo animals commingled with Chinese zodiac creatures. Byrd spotted a blue hippo with pink eyelashes plodding slowly through the grass behind a zebra with an over-stretched neck. A pink elephant with orange tusks lingered in the shadow of a giraffe, stripped of its elegance by gaudy blue spots.

Yet the best scene, which though horrendous amused Byrd most, was found high up in the treetops above the others. Three monkeys with simple cartoon facial expressions sat on uneven branches chattering in the real trees. The one with a happy expression nibbled a banana; another scratched his head in confusion; and a third stared down at the pathway, his paws on his hips in anger suggesting that the passerby was not welcome on his turf below.

The monkey's animated expressions reminded Byrd of the inanimate Hungry Ghost effigies the Zhan family had created. Though trite, their lifelike expressions were surreal and slightly disturbing. They spoke of horror films in which a token clown with a crazed stare peered from high on a bookshelf.

Byrd shivered, "Bala, I think I've seen enough."

"Oh Byrd, one more, it's on the way to something better. I promise. The path crept through a small corridor of trees about twenty feet in length, and then ended abruptly at the edge of a dark though clear lake. A step walkway, made of jumbo round slate stones rising like icebergs above the water, spanned the entire lake.

Halfway across the rock steps, Byrd saw the grand finale of the bizarre cloth concoctions, some sort of indiscernible beast crawling out of the water and up onto one of the slabs with a clawed foot. It licked in voracious delight at the stone with a gangly loose tongue, made of excess cloth that flapped in the breeze. Bala beckoned for Byrd to follow him over the steps toward the beast.

"Byrd, do you know what this is?" He asked when they arrived nearer to the structure.

"Not from this angle, what is it?"

"I'll give you a hint," Bala egged her on, "A Chinese landscape painting wouldn't be complete without one." They jumped from one stone to the next until Byrd stood in front of a fiery eye the size of her head.

"A dragon?" It was the only animal she recalled seeing in a landscape painting.

"Yes! But why a dragon?" Bala held up his hand like an esteemed professor. "According to Granny's Chinese ancestors, the dragon is a reminder that hope and success will always prevail." Bala's eyes reflected off of the glistening water below. He turned to Byrd seriously, "When you don't have anything else to believe in, you put your faith in the dragon.

"The dragon helps us during our darkest hours, Byrd, when clouds obscure the sun and the moon, and typhoon storms rip the delicate shores. Often we can't see the dragon coming to help us in our desperate hour, but he is always there." Bala then turned and continued hopping from one stone to the next.

Fastening her hands to her hips, Byrd halted. "I'm sorry Bala, but that is ridiculous!"

Bala stopped leaping and turned to face her, "What's ridiculous, Byrd?" The genuine expression on his face confused her.

"Tell me, Professor Bala, why should I put my faith in the dragon?" Her sarcasm conveyed mild amusement mixed with moderate annoyance. The gravity of finishing her assignment before catching a flight the following morning started to sink in as the sun sank toward the horizon.

As matter-of-factly as if their conversation had been about the weather Bala suggested, "You should put your faith in the dragon because he knows everything there is to know about Wushu Moon Magic, Byrd." Bala turned and continued hopping along the stones toward the far bank nonchalantly.

Clearly growing frustrated, yet without a keen sense of how to respond to such an earnest though farcical comment, Byrd hollered. "Bala, where are you going!? I thought this was the last one?!"

"It was, but there's one more thing..." His voice trailed off as he leapt further along the stones, leaving Byrd with no choice but to follow.

Byrd tramped from one rock to the next, her shoes slung over her shoulder, until she reached the last rock ending at a small beach cove on an adjoining lake. She leapt and landed between her bottom and her heels on the hot sand. Bala laughed from an old wooden bench nestled in a cluster of dense cattail reeds.

Byrd joined him and slouched onto the bench with a sigh. They looked out at a manmade reservoir, a perfect circular body of water enclosed by a small rocky beach. Though in the distance, a low bridge spanning a dark canal broke its circumference.

Directly in front of them, a lone ruddy boat fit for a single rower lay propped up on a sand dune. Byrd raised her hand to her brow to shade her eyes from direct sunlight and studied the boat's freshly painted façade. Its bow rose in the shape of a stately dragon head while its stern terminated in a broad sweeping tail.

Byrd walked over get a better look at the dragon boat's impressive detailing. Its head was carved then hand-painted in red, blue, green, yellow, black, and white. Beady eyes poked out of sunken sockets, and a thick pink tongue rested in a gaping mouth between two straight rows of teeth. Green nostrils with coarse black hair reminded her of Mu Lian's ponytails at the Chinese opera in Penang. A rounded raised seat made of animal skin and a black paddle with a red blade lay in the dragon's belly.

Byrd walked along the beast's flank toward its tail, scanning the embellished multihued green scales which rolled up in a spiraling pinwheel off the water. The ornate detail of this boat overshadowed the bland boats she'd seen previously. Yet ironically, Byrd found its beauty paled in comparison to the simple crisp folds of the origami boat beached on the altar at the Chu Ang Lu Pagoda in Vietnam. Regardless, she stood by the dragon for some time transfixed by its painstakingly carved details.

When she walked back to the bench, Bala noticed her hunched gait and disconsolate expression. "What's wrong?"

Byrd curled up in a ball on the bench, her toes white from the pressure her hands exerted on their soft flesh.

"Bala, I have to wrap up this assignment, and I'm getting fairly concerned about it. The truth is, though, I know I keep asking you to take me to the final lantern, but I have no idea what I should do when I see it." She started to mumble something about having to 'set the ghosts free,' but stopped when Bala interjected,

"Byrd, what is this assignment you're working on anyway? I asked you on the car-ride but we got cut off..."

Byrd thought about how to respond and eyed Bala sideways. Bala's caring eyes offered comfort, so she began imploringly, "The whole truth and nothing but the truth?"

Bala smiled. "That's right, Byrd." The softness in his eyes suggested that it was okay—safe—to share the entire scope of her assignment.

"I am a photographer, Bala. For years, my boss D. Beak has sent me on assignments to some of the most exotic locales in the world to capture stunning scenery, plants, animals, and people. My work has taken me on Walkabouts with Aboriginal people in Australia, through hallowed ruins locked in Mexican jungles, across the veld in South Africa to photograph leopards stalking impala. You name it. Until recently, I've always been able to live up to the expectations of my boss and I've been fairly satisfied with my work. But recently..." she paused and turned to look at him, "well lately, it seems that the beauty of an iridescent dragon fly fluttering midair or the captivating toothless smile of a little boy won't cut it any more.

"What do you mean they won't cut it?"

"Well, my boss thinks my work is borderline boring, and truthfully, I'm a bit disillusioned by it myself. Though I didn't think I was until I started this assignment. It's ironic, but on this scouting mission, I've felt uninspired by what I've seen."

"Uninspired? But I watched you gazing in on the temple in Georgetown. I saw how much that setting caught your eye. I didn't even know you were a photographer, but I saw how much you yearned to capture the view—if not with a camera—at least with your own eyes."

✓ "Yes, that's true. But that's a beautiful image and easy to photograph. I guess what I'm saying is that I have no way to capture the images that aren't so pleasing to the eye—the ones with struggle, strife, and pain. Take this assignment, I've been chasing ghosts, right? Well, I understand them to symbolize <u>LOSS—lost culture, lost families, lost opportunity, lost love.</u>"

Bala interjected, "Yes, I gathered there was a reason why Tang brought you to the Hungry Ghost Festival."

"Good, so then you know about them."

"Yes, Byrd. Tang is a dear friend, I know all about his ghosts, his family's ghosts, his culture's ghosts..."

"Well, after spending enough time with the Zhan's in Vietnam and then with Tang in Malaysia, I have locked eyes with their ghosts and am disheartened by what I see. Look, I realize that pity won't make ghosts disappear, but I struggle to find compassion for the people who are the instigators behind all of this pain."

Byrd stopped and kicked her feet down into the hot sand. "Look Bala, the last piece of my assignment is to follow the ghosts to the last lantern and set them free. If my heart still hurts from what I've seen, how am I supposed to do that?"

Bala saw the frustration in her eyes. He took a deep breath and answered calmly, "Sounds quite complex and yet pretty simple at the same time." Bala rested his hand on the bench in back of her shoulders.

"What do you mean?" She raised a knee to the bench to face him slightly though continued to look down at the bland sand below.

"Well, I think what you're struggling with is a universal tale but with a personal twist." Byrd waited for him to continue. "We ALL have ghosts Byrd— hidden stories hiding under old scar tissue that we prefer not to share because we don't want others to see. Or we are too scared to face ourselves. Maybe what you need to do is let other's own their ghosts and free your own."

Byrd knew his suggestion was on point. Tang had also alluded to the importance of facing one's own ghosts and letting other people's go. Yet the question remained the same. It's one thing to know to let pity, guilt, anger, fear or pain go; it's another to actually do it. When Byrd remained silent, Bala continued.

"Look Byrd, it's typically only when people are dying or very sick that they have to face what's been lurking in their shadows all along. Take me, for example."

Bala leaned back on the bench and itched his back on a protruding slat. He looked at the lone boat and continued.

"You asked me why I am so joyful. Well, the joy you see now wasn't always there, you know—until I got sick and realized that all the suffering and pain I felt was simply what I gave to it."

"What do you mean by *sick*?" Byrd studied his side profile intently. She noticed for the first time that everything about his face was of average size and proportion, except for his oversized almond eyes.

When he remained silent for a moment, Byrd took a moment to study his profile more carefully. The crow's feet enveloping his eyes were long from many merry occasions and reached deeply into his slick black hair.

Bala turned to face Byrd as directly as he could without shifting his posture. "I am dying, Byrd." Stunned, Byrd's hands released both feet to the ground in a solid thump. Then slowly processing his words, Byrd shook her head in disbelief.

Bala continued, "I have the disease that pokes holes in your small intestine, you can't hold anything in, and slowly you deteriorate. I have a rare form of Crohn's disease."

The conversation shattered in a long silence as a rusty anchor dropped to Byrd's bowels, snagging every other loss she'd felt with it. Byrd's heart ripped in a deep seething tear as she stared at this beautiful man.

She was silent for minutes before speaking. "Bala, I don't know what to say. That hurts my heart so deeply, and I hardly know you. I am so sorry." Byrd stared at Bala's face though couldn't look him in the eye. He must have been quite an extraordinarily handsome man before the disease debilitated his body. She noticed he still was in the face, though the sharpness of his drawn jaw-line now made sense.

Byrd rocked uncomfortably on the bench slats looking directly forward, while Bala sat placidly, following her unsteady movement with his eyes.

"Are you scared to die Bala?"

"No."

"Aren't you sad to have to say goodbye?"

"No."

"Are you angry that this has happened to you?"

"No."

Byrd stopped rocking and looked at him. Bala clasped her hands in his warm palms imploring her not to turn away or fear his eyes. "Byrd, getting sick has helped me to see that all humans are afraid of the same thing—to lose what they love. When it fades—and by that I mean love, faith, belief, hope—they are saddened, hurt, angry—some blame themselves, some blame others. Some become vengeful, others depressed. Yet neither of those solutions make sense. Why? Because they lead you down a dark staircase spiraling up and spiraling down—yet spiraling nowhere."

In the ensuing silence, Byrd began her steady rock again until Bala drew her chin in his direction, gently cupping it with his hand. She stopped rocking and looked at Bala through glassy eyes, emitting a slight smile to counter the sadness she felt.

"Take Tang, for example. He came so close to death on the boat with his family, but he survived. He could have remained embroiled in the ghosts of his past—the grief and sorrow, but no—when you see him, exuberant life jumps from his eyes. Why? Because he has a compassionate soul, filled with so much joy and reverence for everything he experiences. He finds a place for all of it—the good, the bad, and the ugly—in his heart. How? I think it's because he chooses to see things from a perspective other than one tainted by blame, grief or defeat. This is not to say he didn't feel that once. He did, we all do, but there is something beyond that."

Byrd tried to talk, but her words only croaked in her parched throat. She swallowed to moisten her vocal cords and tried again. "When Tang took me to Mu Lian, he tried to differentiate between compassion and pity for me. I understand it logically, yet still, I grapple with it emotionally. It's not easy to unlock some things from your heart, regardless of whether you've been wronged by someone else or hurt someone yourself. Why is that, do you think?"

"Probably because many people have come to understand compassion as the ability to actually feel pain—someone else's or our own—and be at peace with it. In reality, I think that's actually the opposite of what it is. I believe—and think that Tang would probably agree—that compassion is actually about seeing the flip-side of the painful experience. About being able to see what is truly beautiful about something that at first appears dark."

Bala stopped, then characteristic of his simple yet eloquent wisdom, he smiled and added, "Sometimes you need the magic of the moon to illuminate the raw beautiful truth, Byrd."

"Sorry?" Perplexed. Again.

"Come Byrd, let's take a walk around the reservoir. I'll tell you what has helped me." She stood up hesitantly, grabbed his hand and they trudged across the sand.

◐

"When I first learned I was sick, Granny came to visit me. She showed up at my apartment one afternoon, completely unannounced, though I'd spoken with her the day before on the phone. I got home from work to find her on the doorstep of my apartment with a gigantic picnic basket stuffed with mooncakes in her hand. And when I say stuffed, I mean stuffed!" Bala laughed and swung his arms around the invisible barrel at his torso.

"It was around this time of year exactly four years ago that I brought her here. Actually, she suggested it, mentioning something about wanting to see the Chinese Gardens because she had heard there was a special place to sit and eat mooncakes for the Mooncake Festival. As well, she said something about another 'moon festival' that also took place in the park, which she thought I would enjoy.

"Well, I found her comment strange for two reasons. One, we had just learned that my stomach was so weak that I might blow a gasket if I actually ate an entire mooncake myself," he smirked. "And two, I had no idea why Granny from Penang would know anything about some festival celebrations taking place in a park in Singapore." Bala paused, "But we'll get to that."

"Anyway, as a child, Granny used to take me to a park in Georgetown for the festivals at this time of year and we'd eat mooncakes. And year after year, no matter how old or inattentive I got, she'd tell me the story of 6th Sister Yao."

"What's the story of 6th Sister Yao?"

Bala stopped walking and motioned for Byrd to join him on an uneven log in the shade. "Come here, I'll tell you."

"So long story short, Yao was married into a family with a very troubled mother-in-law who asked her to do many unrealistic things—like spin seven jins of thread into silk in a single evening. One night, Yao realized that the task was impossible, even if she spun through the night.

"Nonetheless, Yao desperately wanted to fit into her new family, so she tried her best to spin the silk. Yet halfway through the night, the oil burned out in the candle next to her workstation. Unable to see inside the room's dark interior, Yao gazed forlornly out the window at a trickling ray of light when she spotted the full moon.

"'I'll take my spinner outside and work by the light of the moon!' she thought." Bala did his best female impersonation though it was a tad unrealistic. Regardless, Byrd laughed and he continued.

"So Yao did just that. She walked out the door, set up her workstation and started spinning. Yet halfway through the jins, a great wind swept clouds over the moon and obscured her light. Exhausted and unable to see, she fell asleep under her workbench with tears streaming down her cheeks.

"The next morning when Yao awoke, she had a vague recollection that just before she nodded off, she saw a golden dragon boat sailing through the clouds with a joyful bunch of immortals at the helm. Since the image seemed far too bizarre to be real, Yao believed it was a dream. She climbed out from under the table disconsolately, preparing to face her beastly mother-in-law.

"Yet when she stood up next to the table, she saw that the spinner had turned to gold! And everyone knows what a golden spinner means—that it can turn any amount of silk into heaps of cloth in no time. Yao raced back to the machine and started working again.

By the time her mother-in-law returned, all the jins had been spun into beautiful silk."

Bala looked at Byrd with a wide smile and chuckled, though he halted when he saw her turn away.

"It's a beautiful story Bala, so magical." Byrd folded her arms across her chest looking in the opposite direction.

"But you don't believe it." Bala leaned forward trying to catch her gaze with his eyes.

She uncrossed her arms and looked back at him, then shook her head. "No, Bala. I'm sorry, I don't."

"If it makes you feel better, I didn't either. Until I got sick and Granny added a new twist."

"Okay, so what was the twist?" Byrd couldn't imagine that this surreal tale could have any bearing on reality.

"Well, Granny and I sat right over there," Bala pointed toward the stone walkway and large dragon lumbering out of the far lake. "We sat over there on those stones, under that same dragon, and she spelled it out word-by-word six inches from my face, her eyes locked in mine.

"Granny revealed that the compassionate immortals escaped from a party on the moon in a dragon boat to help when they saw Yao needed it. She also said, and I will never forget this, Byrd, 'They will do the same for you if you believe.'" Bala looked at Byrd earnestly though she sat stiff, still skoptical.

"Believe in what, Bala?"

"I keep telling you Byrd. Please, listen so you can see it—the magic of the moon." For the first time since she had met this charismatic soul, it was Bala's eyes that filled with water. It was Bala who looked away. Yet despite their glossiness, the Indian man smiled.

As Byrd looked at Bala from the side again, she realized that his eyes and his smile were different now, drawing upon a deeper emotion. Bala spanned the water's placid surface casting his gaze into the shimmering pools of sparking sun that chased a warm ray through the reeds on the other side of the reservoir. Byrd followed Bala's eyes into the reeds, as if the source of what he saw would reveal the perception through which he saw it.

"Seriously Bala, what is this magic of the moon you keep referring to?"

Without taking his gaze off the far side of the reservoir, Bala handed Byrd a newspaper clipping from his back pocket. It was smudged and crumbled though still legible. Byrd unfolded the clipping and read the contents highlighted in a box.

*Dear Nomad of the Wind,*

*Shoot for the moon, land in the stars. Stand on a star, get a new view of the moon.*

*Take aim again. This time you have a better idea of what you might actually land upon.*

*As you jump from star to star getting closer to the moon, you may see that it too is real, has holes, and is made of out Swiss cheese.*

*Or it may hold the face of something magical you have never seen before—that is, if you wish upon a star and dare to take aim again.*

*From Crazy Monk of Wushu Moon Pagoda*

A wide though faltering smile spread across Byrd's lips. "But what, I don't understand?!" She looked to Bala for answers.

"I guess someone has been looking out for you, Byrd." He smiled and laughed heart-fully.

"I am baffled, how did the monk know I would be in Singapore? How did you know to give this to me? Do you know the monk?" She had so many questions she didn't know where to begin.

Bala took Byrd's hand in his again and led her back slowly to the far side of the reservoir toward the bench and dragon boat. He filled her in on the perplexing details as they walked.

Apparently Byrd was not the first sojourner to come along seeking lanterns or ghosts in Southeast Asia. Indeed, Bala's explanation made it sound as if there had in fact been many others making the same overland pilgrimage in search of haunting ghouls and bright lights. Some came under the guise of photographers, others authors, an occasional lawyer or businessman, and many intrepid youthful travelers.

Bala also conceded that many of these weary travelers found their way to the Wushu Moon Pagoda to visit the monk—some with the intention of meeting him and others by happenstance. Either way, the number of restless pilgrims who visited the monk had grown so much recently, that finally the monk decided to place a column in the 'Singaporean Times.' This final adage would serve to help guide those who had made the overland journey to Singapore in search of their final destination, but needed a little extra *umph*!

By the time Bala and Byrd rounded the edge of the reservoir back to the dragon boat, Byrd was completely astonished. Bala saw that she yearned for more elucidation.

"Byrd, you are not the only Nomad of the Wind. There are many of you. Many of us, I should say. Many people—guided by lanterns and haunted by ghosts—soul-searching for a way to make sense of our journey and do what serves our best interests without hurting others along the way."

Byrd furrowed her brow and looked at Bala. *Is this some sort of nasty game? Had all of this been a set up? What is going on here?* Byrd was so perplexed by the synchronicity of this encounter, she didn't know what to believe.

"Bala, if what you are saying is true, then how did you know to give me the article? You couldn't have known I met the monk in Vietnam because I never told you! In fact, I didn't mention it to anyone."

"That's true Byrd, but I knew you were searching for lanterns. And I figured it was ghosts that led you to Tang since it was his uncle who introduced you to him. And well, you'll see, but just trust me. I just knew. I've been trying to tell you. It's all about the magic of the moon."

Byrd turned to Bala in frustration. "Bala, I'm sick of hearing that and not understanding what you mean. PLEASE!"

Bala shook his head. "No Byrd, the magic of the moon is different for everyone. I cannot share mine with you. But, I can tell you how I found it."

"Go on," Byrd requested, skeptical though curious.

"Let's just say that your crazy monk friend is onto something. He has a lesson for us all and there is something to that Wushu he speaks of."

"Bala, now I am really confused. How did you know that the monk told me about Wushu?! Now you're scaring me, I don't understand." Byrd stepped back from him, her breathing shallow, eyes dilated and palms sweaty.

Bala saw Byrd was visibly and physically distraught so he clasped her elbows gently in his hands. "It's okay, Byrd. Hang in there." When her breathing slowed again, he continued.

"Byrd, Wushu is an ancient Chinese martial art. Some call it Tai Chi. Others call it shadow boxing. It's what one can use when you don't know what you're fighting, when there is no visible enemy to fight, when there is no one to blame—no one else, not even yourself. It is the practice of this martial art that will help you see the magic of the moon. You must learn to Wushu."

Then to answer her question, Bala added, "The reason I know about Wushu is because the term is intrinsic to my culture. The reason I know the monk mentioned Wushu to you is because ANY monk would mention Wushu...if that makes any sense." He stopped walking and shrugged his shoulders. It seemed that Bala was running out of words too.

"I'm sorry Bala, I know you're trying to help but I have no idea what you are trying to tell me. What the monk was trying to tell me. What Tang was trying to tell me. What Mr. Zhan was trying to tell me. Why D. Beak even sent me on this ridiculous scavenger hunt!" All of Byrd's angst, rage, and fear spouted up from her stomach and spewed out on a sharply pointed arrow aimed directly at Bala.

Though somehow, Bala remained calm. "Byrd, do you ever read Freud?"

"No, are you telling me you do?" Byrd clinched her toes in the gritty hot sand.

"Yes Byrd, I do." He looked at her resolutely. "I remember a book I read in school by Freud. It was called, 'Something something something, and the Shadow Self.' Well, that wasn't the title but you know what I mean."

Byrd put her hands on her hips unreceptive to another explication, but Bala persisted. "Freud suggested that all the parts of you—good and bad—are locked in your unconsciousness, sort of like unruly ghosts who dictate your thoughts whether you know it or not. They are ominously scary and powerfully destructive until we learn to free them. Does that sound like anything else to you?"

Byrd dropped her hands and mumbled, "Sounds a bit like your shadow boxing."

"Precisely! Perhaps you understand Freud better than Wushu because his philosophy comes from your own western culture. But the point remains the same —eastern or western. Unless we can learn to free our ghosts, or our shadow selves—whatever lurks wherever inside of us—will always haunt us."

Bala paused, then continued, "Byrd, there is a reason why your culture talks of skeletons in the closet, you know." He smiled, which brought a smile to Byrd's face. *He certainly has a way of communicating precariously complex topics with lighthearted simplicity.*

Then Bala's expression turned serious again, "Byrd, you MUST practice Wushu to set your ghosts free."

Byrd looked down at the ground obstinately. "Bala, I get it. This isn't about the overseas Chinese ghosts, this isn't about a cultural ghost, a familial ghost, your ghosts. I know you've been trying to suggest that I have to face my own ghosts. And for that matter, we all have to face our own ghosts rather than each other's. I get that."

Byrd continued, "And I know you are telling me that I must practice Wushu to do that. And I understand that supposedly *if* I do, I will see the magic of the moon. And that *then*, I will see the lanterns and the ghosts for what they truly are. But THAT is a very tall order."

Byrd looked at him anxiously. "Bala how am I supposed to do all of that by the time I board my airplane tomorrow? The sun is setting, I still haven't seen the last lantern," she wanted to continue but stopped. She was just too tired. Instead, her eyes glossed over and she looked at Bala—expressionless. Bala matched her expression, then abruptly, he walked away. Byrd winced.

*Great, now I'm losing my friend too.*

Bala walked over to the dragon boat and unhitched the boat from a wooden post. His back curved under its weight as he lugged the heavy stern over large jagged rocks and shimmied the boat into the water to float freely. Byrd watched the dragon's tail slither on the shimmering surface.

"Where are you going?" she asked.

"It's not where I'm going, it's where you're going."

"Where is that?"

"Well, as you say, it's getting late—he looked at the setting sun over Byrd's shoulder. I have to get home and you have to finish your assignment."

"Hop in." Byrd gave him a curious look. "This dragon will take you out to the sea through that canal." Bala pointed toward the bridge on the far side of the reservoir. "This is your ticket to the last lantern, Byrd."

Byrd stood eager yet anxious. "But Bala, I'm not ready. I don't know what I'll do when I see it. I can't..."

"It's time, Byrd." Bala steadied the boat with a furrowed brow. She looked at him and realized he was right. She had to say goodbye. Byrd walked to the boat meekly, her steps felt weightless as the sand sifted through her toes. She sunk one foot into the boat's slimy belly covered in pond scum and rooted the other into the sand. Bala released the gangly rope from his hand and stepped toward Byrd.

He wrapped her up in a long embrace and caressed the back of her neck with his hand. Byrd had forgotten how comforting it felt to be held during the solitary months of her assignment. Her thigh muscles trembled as the boat started to sway with the water and the distance between her legs widened. Neither spoke.

Finally, when her gait stretched as far as she could manage, Byrd released Bala's embrace. Cautiously she clamored into the boat, one hand on either side of the dragon's thick girth. Once she settled herself on the seat, Bala gently pushed the boat out of the sand and it stuttered into the water before floating freely.

As she lifted the paddle and wiped its damp handle on her leg, Bala called out, "Wait, take this in case you get hungry!" Bala hawked a shiny red object through the air. It landed in the boat in a single plunk. Byrd looked down to find the fourth uneaten mooncake resting in the belly of the boat. She laughed joyfully though fought tears.

Byrd glided backwards steadily, splashing her face to conceal her wet cheeks. When Byrd and Bala's prolonged waves reached a sullen awkwardness, Byrd plunged the paddle fully into the water on her right side and reared the dragon head directly toward the bridge.

Byrd leaned into the center of the boat, her lower body cocked forward on the seat. With her gaze focused inward, she shifted her upper body so that it hovered over the boat's starboard side. She stretched forward at a 45 degree angle and plunged the paddle 90 degrees into the water. Her rickety stroke dropped two feet and tracked through the water, until it lingered behind her back. She lifted the paddle into the air, then dropped it into the water on the opposite side to glide straight forward.

She moved slowly through the water until she reached the bridge. She looked over her shoulder one more time for Bala, who stood on the bench waving enthusiastically. Fanning the sky with her paddle, Byrd gave him one final wave, then slipped into the shadow of the bridge.

A winged animal fluttered above Byrd as she reached the middle of the bridge's sinewy darkness, then flew out of the cavernous tunnel flapping madly into the sky. It startled her and the ghosts came whizzing back.

Grotesquely deranged shadows—her fears of facing this next portion of her journey alone, of never understanding D. Beak's clues, not finding the last lantern or setting the ghosts free—all of it floated in the murky stagnant water under the bridge. Byrd gagged in the smelly dank air, choking on her own fumes.

She sat exhausted, nearly unable to paddle toward the light emanating on the bridge's far side. Fortunately, a slight lunar tide rose up from the sea at the canal's far terminus and lured her forward. As the boat continued forward at a snail's pace out from under the bridge, a steady beam of late afternoon light danced on the dragon's nose, pierced his eyes, and finally perked his ears. It draped his dark back in a warm colorful glow.

Byrd heard Bala's words in her ears, "This is your ticket to the last lantern. But you MUST practice Wushu to set your ghosts free." When the sun crept up her knees, Byrd dropped the paddle over the port side of the boat and let the blade dredge up a seedling of hope. She raised her head and caught brief sight of the long tunnel breaking a grove of coniferous trees in half on its way out to sea. She righted the dragon's head to gaze directly up the long narrow canal and began her voyage to the last lantern.

Byrd's first stroke hit the open waterway with a vivacious slap. Miniscule tidal currents swiveled the paddle in the middle of her elongated stroke. She lifted the blade out of the water and paused for a split second, then punched the paddle forcefully forward through the air.

She dropped it straight back down again, her bottom hand drifting through the frigid water. Finally when she couldn't retract any further, she whipped the paddle back, her back muscles gliding into neutral position. Starboard to port. Port to starboard.

Byrd counted out-loud—fifteen short explosive strokes—to gain momentum and raise the dragon's head out of the water. When the dragon's lower lip hovered just above its surface, she counted fifteen more strokes—these longer and more tedious—to gain distance. In a final push before her muscles relented, Byrd paddled fifteen more short chops to gain a few extra feet then grunted like a long-over due mother in labor.

Deep breaths rejuvenated the depleting strokes. Though she was alive with wretched feelings—fear, anger, and sadness catapulted her into swift motion.

In time she found a steady rhythm with a powerful stroke. She felt out of her body, an observer in her own terrain and watched from the shore. Her forearms and shoulders locked into a rigid triangular shape, her inner elbow cocked toward the center of the boat. Byrd made mental notes of every action. Determinedly, she paddled forward in swift counts toward the sea.

Finally, her knee became raw from digging into the sideboards, so she paused for a moment to rest, raising her head for the first time since entering the canal. A sliver of moonlight crept up from the sea.

Sinewy cracks molested its pure surface as it rose gainfully into the sky. By the time she approached the canal's end, it hovered midway between air and sea, and the moon's strong tidal current rocked the boat sideways in the open water. Yet still, not a lantern in sight.

Byrd screamed, This is bogus, a wild goose-chase with no end! Staring out at a widely expansive sea and a burgeoning moonscape, Byrd saw disillusionment baiting her—hook, line, and sinker. Her heart sunk, imagining that she would have to return home in the dark, with little understanding of the lanterns, ghosts, dragons or Wushu. Worse still, a failed assignment and a compromised livelihood doing what she loved more than anything else in the world—capturing images.

In that moment, Byrd stopped rowing [paddling] completely. She dropped the paddle into the boat and sunk down into its slimy depths. She closed her eyes and rested her head on the soft skin of the drum seat. A single tear dribbled down her cheek and tickled her neck. She shivered and her muscles began to ache from the weight of her head wobbling on the seat.

Grief coated her tongue and she couldn't spit it out. It left a nasty putrid aftertaste in her mouth and hung her tongue out to dry. There were no more words, no clues, no imagery, just pure evocative feelings swarming in the boat.

On previous occasions, Byrd had reached for her camera, a pen, or a friend to try to make sense of what she saw. Yet here at the end of the canal staring out at the sea alone, there was nothing to do but to feel what rumbled inside. And it felt awful, so she sat up—restless.

She heaved herself up onto the seat. Elbows cocked on her knees with her head in her hands, she rolled her neck around in sweeping circles left to right, then down to release the tension in her spine. She circled her head in this fashion for some time until, it too, got tired. Finally, she tilted her head up and opened her eyes.

It was then that she spotted the full Harvest moon erupting from the ocean. It shimmered on the water like glistening frosting on a chocolate molten lava cake.

Byrd gasped, studying its perfect crisp circumference. Its glossy surface was yellow—the color of saffron rice—but for a few distinctly darker splotches. Byrd recalled that the full Harvest moon was notably larger than other full moon's because it occurred in the fall when the moon was actually closest to the earth. This glowing ball was proof!

And yet, despite its arresting rapture, Byrd's heart still hurt. She didn't see any magic when she looked at it. No dragon boats or mysterious immortals flying out of it either. Not that she truly believed they were coming anyway...

*Yes, Bala, it certainly is intrinsically beautiful, but only a fool would believe in Wushu Moon Magic.*

Byrd settled back into her mummy position in the dragon's belly and closed her eyes, letting the moon's tide nudge her backward—back to land empty-handed.

Byrd was startled from a semiconscious state when the boat's stern hit the canal's edge with a jarring jolt. She rubbed her eyes, edging sleep from their corners, and wondered how long she'd been asleep. She looked up from her horizontal position in the boat's hull and into the shadow of creepy sinewy boughs hanging over the canal.

Then her eye caught something odd—a dim flickering light hanging from a low-hanging branch. She sat up and briskly edged herself onto her seat. Grabbing the paddle, she pushed the boat away from the canal bank and glided sideways until it floated directly under the glowing object.

Impossible! A simple red lantern—round and hollow in the center—swayed above with a tiny candle burning at its metal base. As if that weren't strange enough, within moments, it seemed that the lantern's light grew stronger. Perplexed, Byrd glanced left to right, up and down, and then finally toward the sea. A large plumy cloud sat heavily in the sky, covering half of the full Harvest moon. Though as the cloud rolled gently off of the blazing ball, the entire sky brightened.

Byrd swiveled her gaze from the moon back to the lantern directly above. Now fully ablaze by the light of the moon's reflection off its tiny flame, the lantern illuminated the entire hull of her boat and all the water within a five foot circumference below it. She looked up, captivated.

Finally, Byrd's neck began to cramp, so she dropped her gaze toward the reservoir and was even more stunned by the light she saw ahead. An entire trail of blazing lanterns—maybe 15 though she lost count—spanned the entire length of the canal back to the bridge.

The globes swung gently from branches overhanging the narrow swath of water. Smiling at the little orbs dangling from the trees she thought of Bala. Yes, I see it now my friend. *The magic of the moon. It's reflective luminescence is what magnifies the lantern's light.* **Yet still, she wondered,** *How had she not noticed the lanterns before?*

It occurred to Byrd that she had never actually looked up into the branches of the trees, as her focused gaze remained fixed down while traversing the canal. Then again without the moon's reflection earlier in the day, they probably would have been hard to see anyway. Now, they were impossible to miss!

Byrd redirected the boat so that its bow faced the reservoir again and she coasted forward through the canal. As the moon rose higher in the sky, each lantern glowed more brilliantly than the last.

As the dragon boat lunged rhythmically through the canal and slowed to a crawl near the bridge, Byrd dipped her hands into the cool water. She felt the slimy bellies of pond shrubs underneath the surface and tugged at them gently, lulling the boat to a standstill.

Byrd groped her way hand-over-hand through the reeds to a muddy bank where her fingers tore into its mucky soil. The moist mud squished through her fingers and slipped under her nails. She wrapped her hands around a small tree trunk and hoisted herself onto the squishy shore.

She tied the boat's noose around the tree trunk and shimmied up the bank toward the bridge. Finding its cement embankment with her fingers, she hoisted herself up onto its cool hard surface.

It was then that she spotted the most elaborate display of lanterns she'd ever seen—the entire Chinese Garden was aglow! Each cartoon caricature basking in the luminescence of moonbeams bouncing off of their reflective Teflon sheen!

The moon shot rays toward the blue hippo with pink eyelashes, the zebra with an oversized neck, and the pink elephant with rounded tusks. And as the moonlight reflected off of the tiny lights adorned to each of the animal's wire frames wrapped in shiny Teflon cloth, the animals glowed brilliantly!

Bright moon bolts pierced the treetops where the monkey's sat, illuminating their frozen movements, stirring them to fantastical life. Flowers and birds of all shapes and sizes radiated like colorful lights down a Las Vegas boulevard, the likes of which she'd shunned in the daylight.

Even Snow White, with her oversized basket and tacky garb, beckoned to Byrd. All of nature's kingdom—humans, animals, and plants—came to life as moonbeams cascaded into the park. Byrd witnessed the most magical sight she had ever seen dazzle in the night.

She crawled on top of the bridge's stone sidewall and glanced up at the sky, her eyes readjusting to the dark. Sparkling stars strung together as constellations dotted the pitch-black night. Immediately, she thought of the crazy monk's newspaper clipping and folded its verse into the fabric of her assignment.

She shot for the moon the day she agreed to D. Beak's assignment and ventured out to find her first lantern. She landed in the stars—amidst the shiny red lanterns of Ho Chi Minh City's Chinatown. Finally after a month of searching for elusive ghosts, she came face to face with them at the pagoda on the eve of the Hungry Ghost Festival. Though they weren't what she expected, she left Ho Chi Minh City with a sense of who they truly were—lost souls sailing in a sea of suffering. Next she calibrated her search with a better understanding of the ghosts and took aim at her next clue.

Landing on the next star—a mecca of lanterns in the Meeting Place of Asia, she learned about the myth of Mu Lian with Tang in Georgetown. He helped her to see that through compassion—not pity or vengeance—that ghosts can be freed.

Standing from this star, Byrd took aim a final time for the City by the Sea. Here she found the final ghost when she met the Grim Reaper of love and hope—the mortality of humanity—in the eyes of Bala. And Bala, with all of his reverence showed Byrd who the ghosts truly were—the shadow of ourselves. As mystical and strange as the journey had been—it was real and had holes just like Swiss cheese—as the crazy monk's adage had alluded to. Yet still, there was more...

*What else was there to see? The last line of the monk's column suggested that the moon may hold the face of something magical if we dare to take aim again.*

Byrd stood up and walked toward the farthest side of the bridge leading back to shore. A small billboard listing ongoing events at the Chinese Gardens hung in the center of a large cork board. A poster suggested that the park was open for extra hours during the week of September 21. Byrd recalled that her flight departed Singapore on September 22, so that made today September 21. *But what was going on?*

Byrd continued to scroll through the poster's contents which revealed that some of the Mid-Autumn Full Moon Festival activities would be taking place here in the park, while other activities took place in the city central. A bullet-point list of those activities at the park included a mooncake-eating contest and a lantern-making contest.

She continued reading the background information on the poster and learned that the Chinese Mid-Autumn Full Moon Festival actually drew upon two distinct celebrations—the Mooncake Festival and the Lantern Festival. Though there was one common ingredient. A full Harvest moon!

Finally it hit her. Byrd recalled what Bala had said about Granny's interest in two festivals at the **Chinese Gardens.** *Of course, now I see! Those tacky caricatures in the park—gaudy lawn ornaments by day and lanterns by night! So Bala knew all along that leading me to the mooncakes would lead me to the lanterns!*

Byrd laughed to herself and grinned widely as she stepped back from the sign post and wandered across the bridge toward the embankment. As she shuffled down the hill toward the canal to retrieve her boat, she hastily recalled her final clue. *'At the last of the string of lanterns, capture the Hungry Ghosts and set them free.'*

After Byrd clamored back into the boat, she released her grip from the shore and let the boat glide gently back toward the middle of the canal. Her legs flopped loosely in the boat, nearly overextending her knees.

*Now what, how will I set them free?*

Her right foot skidded stiffly on something underneath her shoe, so Byrd lifted her toe and peered underneath. Byrd picked up the crushed mooncake and unwrapped it slowly.

She flattened the thin crumpled paper, and held it up to the moonlight, studying the opaque moon image imprinted on its surface. The real moon cast a warm glow on the red paper and filtered through its delicate surface—outlining a faint replica of the paper moon on her lap.

Immediately, Byrd had an idea—perhaps a way to let the ghosts go using her own variation of Wushu. She dug into her pocket for the ink-stone from the monk and unwound the calligraphy brush from her hair.

Byrd smoothed the red paper against her knee, dipped the inkblot in the canal and set it on the seat beside her. She dabbed the brush in the black ink and blotted it against her shirt sleeve. She dropped the brush to the red paper and stopped, noticing the shadow of her hand lingering on the page in front of her unwritten word.

*Ah, so the moon has finally illuminated you too! Byrd entertained her own ghost with a playful laugh. I completely forgot that ghosts are nocturnal too, but I guess we're all at the mercy of a beautiful moon!*

So by the light of the full Harvest moon, Byrd steadied her brush until the words found themselves and she chased her shadow across the page in ten lines that reflected the journey.

After she reread the lines and was certain they were what she wished to convey, she dropped the brush. Exhausted she laid down in the hull of the boat. Byrd rubbed her taut finger muscles and wept quietly—not sad tears, just tears of release.

When her glassy eyes cleared, she cocked her head to the side where an object rolled toward her nose with the water lulls below. It was an empty plastic Coke bottle, undoubtedly pitched haplessly by a previous rower.

Normally Byrd hated to see litter—it bothered her even more to think of modernization creeping into this foreign land—but this time there was something intriguing about the bottle. *What else could the bottle be besides litter?* Byrd sat up startled, hearing Bala in her head: 'It's hard for Westerner's to understand the magic of Wushu because the idea isn't embedded within your culture. I guess what I am trying to say is try to see things from a new view, Byrd. Shake things up a bit, look upside down.' She smiled.

*Well, here is a universal image—whether I like it or not—probably more recognizable than anything else on this planet.* **Byrd chuckled,** *It would never be the image I envisioned 'capturing' my eye for this photo assignment, but it is universal enough for everyone to comprehend.*

Byrd wound her note like a scroll and dropped it into the bottle where it unwound itself snug against the bottle's cylindrical shape. She sealed the bottle tightly with the teeth-marked cap, then dropped it into the water where it bobbed like a buoy on the shimmering surface.

And finally, Byrd SAW the last lantern. The materials had been with her all along, but it wasn't until she looked at them under the right light, that she realized she had to piece them together herself to set her own ghosts free.

When the moon filtered through the shiny red paper and reflected her dark brush strokes, Byrd smiled. Litter turned treasure—universal turned personal—myth made real—her little red lantern a new twist on an old tale.

Before redirecting the dragon's head back under the bridge, Byrd read the words a final time. The script was simple—nearly childish—but the message was clear and what she wished to say. Byrd laughed out loud. It turned out that D. Beak—with her puzzling poetics—had been a woman after her own heart all along. And Byrd's first attempt at Wushu read...

---

WUSHU MOON MAGIC

moonlight illuminates fiery lanterns and shadowy ghosts.
it's so easy to forget that it doesn't matter which we meet,
if we leap with wushu, we see both are steps to growth.

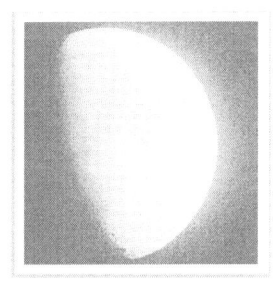

this means plunging into murky mekong's
and the southern china sea
with COMPASSION for ourselves and each other—
wushu will illuminate the flip-side & reveal what it may truly be
FINALLY
—a surefire way to steer the dragon boat
toward what we wish to see

---

And then, there was the pending photo assignment:

A new image unfolded in Byrd's mind. The photo-essay would began much like it had from day one, with the forlorn face of a little girl. Though this time the girl would be sitting on the bank of a river—perhaps somewhere in Africa or South America or Iceland for that matter.

She would spot a shiny red bottle bobbing in the water with curious words in another language flickering in the moonlight. She would fetch it and bring the mysterious bottle home to her parents wondering what it was. They would have a strange explanation for bizarre foreign cultures sending messages in bottles.

The girl would grow up curious about these strange cultures, and one day when she left home, she would embark on a journey through a new land to find her own. When she returned home, she would realize that it wasn't that different after all. That is to say, the journey was just the same as anyone else's, anywhere else—lit by lanterns and haunted by ghosts—until she chose her own form of Wushu to set the ghosts free.

As the dragon boat slipped back under the bridge, Byrd rubbed her sore eyes thinking that she would sleep well on the return flight home. Her eyes needed a break before getting behind a fresh lens the next day.